"Honey, Why Deprive a Fellow of His Fun?"

"I'm not your honey, and I'm not here for you to have fun with!" Lacy snapped.

"No?" The deep-set eyes narrowed and Lacy shivered as the sun went behind the low bank of clouds on the horizon. "I didn't hear you making any qualifying conditions when you begged me to take you aboard yesterday. In fact, if I remember correctly, you said you'd fight tooth and nail if I tried to put you ashore. Changed your mind?"

She was entirely too close to all that masculinity. She could feel the heat radiating from him, and she reached out a hand to push herself away.

"What's the matter, honey—afraid I may take undue liberties?"

DIXIE BROWNING
is a native of North Carolina, and many of her stories are born as she travels from her home in Winston-Salem to her cottage in Frisco, on Hatteras Island. She is also an accomplished watercolor artist, as well as a writer.

Dear Reader:

I'd like to take this opportunity to thank you for all your support and encouragement of Silhouette Romances.

Many of you write in regularly, telling us what you like best about Silhouette, which authors are your favorites. This is a tremendous help to us as we strive to publish the best contemporary romances possible.

All the romances from Silhouette Books are for you, so enjoy this book and the many stories to come. I hope you'll continue to share your thoughts with us, and invite you to write to us at the address below:

Editor-in-Chief,
Silhouette Books,
P.O. Box 910,
517 Lorne Ave.,
Stratford, Ontario N5A 6W3

DIXIE BROWNING
Loving Rescue

Silhouette *Romance*

Published by Silhouette Books New York

Distributed in Canada by PaperJacks Ltd., a Licensee
of the trademarks of Simon & Schuster, a division of
Gulf+Western Corporation.

For Lee—remember?

SILHOUETTE BOOKS, a Simon & Schuster Division of
GULF & WESTERN CORPORATION
1230 Avenue of the Americas, New York, N.Y. 10020
In Canada distributed by PaperJacks Ltd.,
330 Steelcase Road, Markham, Ontario.

Copyright © 1982 by Dixie Browning

Distributed by Pocket Books

ISBN: 0-671-57191-5

First Silhouette Books printing December, 1982

10 9 8 7 6 5 4 3 2 1

Map by Ray Lundgren

Printed in Canada

Chapter One

Small clouds, like gilt-edged shadows, drifted across the cerulean sky, and Lacy shivered in spite of the eighty-degree heat. The breeze, so light that it barely moved the stiff fronds of coconut palms, brought a drift of flowery fragrance to the sordid neighborhood, adding a further note of unreality to the situation in which she found herself. Instead of a dream vacation, Lacy felt as if she had wandered into a nightmare.

It was hard to say just when the dream had begun to go sour. They had been told there was a message for Carolyn as soon as they disembarked and then went through the frustration of locating the man who had taken it down. Lacy, keyed up for weeks in anticipation of the long-awaited trip to Belize, found it impossible to sustain her excitement as she followed Carolyn from one minor official to another, each seemingly with less English than the last.

The message was finally located—Carolyn's mother

had fallen and broken her hip and was in the hospital and Carolyn was needed at home. That had been bad enough, although Carolyn had taken it with characteristic good humor, refusing to allow Lacy to consider going home with her. Lacy had stayed to watch her friend depart, staring at the jet as it was quickly enveloped in shimmering heat waves. Only then did she turn away to face the fact that for the first time in her life, she was totally on her own in a strange country, among people who spoke a different language, and she didn't know a single soul.

You're twenty-two years old—a college graduate, for Pete's sake! She waited with increasing nervousness for a customs official to come and see her through the last barrier. They had done their duty and disappeared while Lacy and Carolyn were busy tracking down the message and arranging Carolyn's return flight.

The hollow feeling inside her expanded as she watched the last of her fellow travelers disappear through the swinging glass doors. They were French—a honeymoon couple, judging from the languishing looks and touches that passed between them. Lacy sighed wistfully. Her French was even less adequate than her high school Spanish—strictly classroom variety and not up to deciphering the dialect she had heard from all the airport personnel. There wasn't another tourist in sight when the customs official finally strolled into view to check her one suitcase and her borrowed backpack.

At this rate she wasn't going to have much time for sight-seeing before she boarded the bus in the morning to go on to Tikal, where she and Carolyn had planned to join a group of other teachers. Struggling with her two bags, heavy with all the things Aunt Lottie had insisted she take just to be on the safe side, she pushed open the door and squinted against the late-afternoon sun.

A small, shambling man separated himself from among several leaning up against the row of dilapidated automobiles. "Taxi?" he inquired with an obsequious duck of his head.

Lacy, bracing herself against a sudden feeling of misgiving, repeated the name of her hotel several times, and the man nodded and grabbed her bags from her hands. She looked helplessly over her shoulders in the direction Carolyn's plane had taken off, as if seeking reassurance, but there was no help there. She was on her own—timid, mousy Lacy Davis, the original small-town girl, who had never traveled outside her own state of North Carolina except for a weekend in Washington with her high school senior class.

As they rattled along a potholed road through miles of uninspired countryside, Lacy watched the fine cloud of dust drift into the open car windows and settle on everything, including her once-white jeans, bought especially for the trip. Aunt Lottie had warned her against traveling in white, but ever since she had known about the trip she had been dreaming the most ridiculous dreams. Her overactive imagination had taken all the glamorous, exotic advertisements for bathing suits, or suntan lotion, or perfume, and woven a fantasy from them.

She had seen her unremarkable self, Lacy Aurelia Davis, schoolteacher-to-be, somehow metamorphosed into a svelte, tanned creature with long, sunstreaked hair and mysterious emerald eyes, instead of a very ordinary girl with medium brown hair, freckles, and eyes that were neither gray nor green. She'd be dressed in white jeans and perhaps a red halter, something casually twisted together from a scarf and a string of wooden beads. She'd be barefooted, of course, with her blond hair streaming in the wind as her head rested on the broad, tanned shoulder of her faceless, nameless lover.

In her fantasy they were strolling romantically along the Techincolor shores of San Pedro, like the couple in the travel brochure.

Instead she was being driven further and further from anything that looked faintly like an exotic tropical vacation land by a disreputable-looking man in a rattletrap of a car—a shady-looking creature whose grasp of English had quickly gone from an unlikely Oxford accent with a south-of-the-border cadence to zilch. Nothing. *No habla!*

"This can't be the way," she declared in a small, squeaky voice.

The man shrugged and cut his eyes at her by way of a rearview mirror that was partly obscured by a suggestive decal and a six-inch sombrero that dangled from one side.

"I think you'd better take me back to the airport," she ordered with all the authority she could summon. Something was wrong—dreadfully wrong. This couldn't be Belize City—there was no sign of any hotel, much less the one her travel agent assured her was the best available in the coastal town.

The car swerved recklessly up to a filthy-looking building of some sort and, without bothering to shut off the engine, the man slid out from under the wheel. He opened her door, giving it the extra kick required to unlatch it, and Lacy gripped the seat, not at all certain she wanted to leave the comparative safety of the car. This was not right, she thought in growing panic. If only Carolyn . . .

And then he reached for her, his hands pudgy and none too clean, and she scampered out the other door, glaring at him across the dusty top of the ramshackle car. "All right! But I certainly don't intend to pay you for—"

He didn't wait for her to finish. He jumped back into

the car and took off, throwing up a cloud of dust that obscured not only the license plate, but the car as well. Lacy exhausted the small store of profanity at her command as she wondered how she was going to retrieve her luggage. It took several minutes for her to realize that that had been the whole intent of the charade—and that she had left her purse in the car as well.

And by then, of course, it was too late. She was frozen to the pale, dusty earth. A trickle of perspiration crept down her spine under the hot mulberry-colored sweater she wore over her jeans. It had been chilly this morning when she had left home, and she had planned to change on the plane, but somehow she had never got around to it.

A feeble voice kept whispering insider her head: the police! She had to find the police—someone, *anyone* who could help her, could wake her up from this horrid nightmare and get her onto a plane headed home. She didn't care if she never saw Tikal, didn't care if she never got to San Pedro to walk the lovely, tropical beach with a dream man.

A glint of light broke through the numb terror that held her immobile and she turned her head slowly, like an old woman. A man had come out of what seemed to be a garage of some sort and he hesitated, as if trying to make up his mind about something.

There was something in the set of the shoulders, in the angle of the head, that made her move a hesitant step in his direction. And then her uncertainty gave way to panic and she ran, intent only on closing the distance between her and the man, who had turned to stare at her enigmatically through mirrored sunglasses.

An hour later Lacy was curled up defensively on a berth aboard a sloop named the *Phoenix*. She knew absolutely nothing about boats—still less about the man, who told her only that his name was Jordan Stone. She had simply taken a look at those shoulders and the commanding set of his head and homed in on him as if he were the north star and she a lost mariner.

"Do you speak English?" That had been her first frantic question, and between the panting and the shivering she had despaired of making herself understood.

"Yes." The clipped voice told her nothing, nor did the mocking reflection from those glasses, but at least he had stood there while she got her breath.

It was all she could do to restrain herself from hanging around his neck, but she stood her ground as she stammered out her story. "My purse—my luggage —all my money and m-my tickets and everything," she wailed. Flinging out an arm, she had pointed toward where the taxi had disappeared. "How can I find them? I have to get them back and I don't speak Spanish, and m-my friend's gone, and . . ."

The rains had come then, one of those sudden, unannounced showers that sweep in from the Caribbean, and it was the last straw. Lacy felt something inside her give way and then the hot tears were joining the warm rain to streak down her dusty cheeks as she stood there, staring helplessly up at the man before her. Those frustrating glasses—that aggressive chin! Why didn't he *say* something?

"W-would you please take your g-glasses off?"

After only the briefest hesitation, he obliged her, and she took a deep, shuddering breath at the sight of a pair of reassuringly steady eyes. They were blue—the color of the Caribbean of her daydreams—and she was suddenly extremely glad.

Not that they looked overjoyed at the moment. If she had been concerned with her ego, she'd have been finished off by the expression on that lean, rather haughty face. He looked as if he had impulsively fished a kitten out of the river in spite of the fact that he didn't care for the species, and now he didn't quite know what to do with it.

She was past caring. Frightened, alone, filthy, and getting wetter by the minute, she allowed him to take her arm and direct her toward the waterfront. "Come on. We'll sort you out somewhere where it's drier, at least."

The somewhere had turned out to be the *Phoenix,* out of New Orleans. As far as Lacy was concerned, it spelled security. Sturdy, a little the worse for wear, it struck her as an incredibly beautiful sight. He had propelled her through the door that she later came to know as a hatch, down three steps into a compact, all-purpose room paneled in teak and holly and furnished with an assortment of stainless steel appliances. She was pleasantly surprised at the cleverness of the interior design, but mostly she just felt an enormous relief. As she sank down on a comfortably padded locker, she was shaken by a hard shudder as the last of her nightmare ebbed away. Only now did she realize that she had been on the very edge of hysteria.

His name was Jordan Stone and he was sailing north, with New Orleans as his eventual destination. He was sailing alone.

"Maybe you could use a—a crew?" She wrapped her hands around the steaming mug of coffee that he had provided, unasked.

The intensely blue eyes took a thorough inventory of her, from her inexpensive sneakers, now stained with dust, to the once-white jeans and the hot mulberry sweater. She could feel the heat prickling her neck and she knew her face would be flushed with it, making her freckles stand out as pale spots on her cheeks and nose.

Somewhere along the way she had lost the scarf that had tied her hair back in what she liked to think of as a sophisticated style. The steamy rain had turned her barely manageable waves into a wild crop of corkscrew curls.

So all right! She wasn't pretty—she had never claimed to be. But she wasn't an ogre either! He was taking his own sweet time about making up his mind and unfortunately she was in no position to complain.

"You're an experienced sailor?" he finally asked, when she had been about ready to scream.

To lie or not to lie. Lacy had never set foot on a boat before, but if she admitted to being so much dead weight, then she might find herself out in the cold— figuratively speaking. And if it wasn't all that cold, at least it was dark, foreign—and utterly frightening. She was determined not to move from this snug haven until it was safely moored in the United States. She prevaricated. "North Carolina has scads of water—lakes, sounds, oceans—well, at least one—and I'm an excellent cook," she added hopefully. That was no lie, at least. She had helped her aunt with the teachers' boardinghouse since she was thirteen and Aunt Lottie's cooking was what kept the teachers coming back year after year.

"You've got no papers, no passport, no clothes, no money, and you don't speak the language," Jordan summed up discouragingly. "You don't know a soul, your friend has deserted you, and you're stupid enough to want to sail alone with a man you don't know a thing about—I could be a criminal, for all you know." His tone was contemptuous and Lacy instinctively tried to make herself smaller.

"If you're trying to frighten me," she said in a voice that sounded bolder than she felt, "then you're wasting your time. I'm already so petrified that if I move fast I'll

14

shatter in a million pieces, and nothing you can say to me is going to budge me from this boat. I'll hang on with teeth and toenails if you try to put me out now. I'll scream my head off and—"

"Take it easy—nobody's going to jettison you. There's an extra berth, little more than a closet, but I don't suppose you'll take up all that much room. I plan to cast off in half an hour, though, and I warn you, if you're in any big rush to get home, you'd better get out and walk. I'm planning to break my trip at Isla Mujeres, and depending on any one of several factors, I may be there as long as a week."

"Just get me away from here," Lacy managed through teeth that were chattering again. It was pure tension—a reaction to everything that had happened to her since leaving home in the early hours of dawn. The temperature still hovered somewhere in the middle seventies in spite of the sporadic showers, but she was chilled clear through and it was going to take more than a mug of coffee to warm her up again.

Not that she was frightened of Jordan Stone. The man was obviously no seagoing hobo. One had only to see the way he walked, as if he owned the very earth, to hear the authoritative timbre of his deep voice to know he was a man of substance, one accustomed to issuing orders and having them obeyed.

A small, wary portion of her brain whispered that the lethal combination of tough good looks and inbred arrogance could be extremely dangerous to a woman— but then, it was obvious that he didn't look on her as a woman. She was excess baggage, a nuisance, which suited her fine. She had made it a policy all her life to steer clear of temptation, but these, as someone had once said, were perilous times.

"All right, then," Jordan Stone remarked, looking down at where she was curled up in a tight knot on the locker, "suppose you get out of those wet things and shower the mud off. I'll show you your room and how to work the head—" At her look of perplexity, he tilted a mocking brow at her. "Sorry, mate—the bathroom," he said with heavy sarcasm. "Then maybe you can turn a hand in the galley and get us a meal. I'm going to run out through the reef before it gets dark and we'll lay over for the night off English Cay Light and make an early start in the morning."

Lacy washed her hair and showered off in the compact head before it occurred to her that she didn't have anything to change into, and she eyed her damp, dusty jeans and sweater distastefully. Then, hearing that firm tread on the deck overhead, she opened the door to the other cabin and looked about her curiously. With a towel draped around her, she opened the door to the narrow locker.

Whoever Jordan Stone was, he did himself proud when it came to a wardrobe. Dinner jacket, black silk worsted pants, a tropical-weight suit, several sets of khakis, and a safari jacket. There were two coarsely woven cotton outfits consisting of drawstring trousers and a hooded, pullover shirt with kangaroo pocket in front, and it was one of these that she helped herself to, holding it up and deciding that, yes, it would do nicely.

On an impulse she couldn't explain, she opened a drawer and saw neat rows of socks and briefs. Fascinated by the variety of colors—she had thought, if she had considered the subject at all, that men's underwear came only in white—she slammed the drawer shut.

Not a moment too soon. At a noise behind her she spun about, clutching the towel as she felt a blush start at her toes and work its way up to her hairline.

"I came down to offer you something to wear. Help yourself," he mocked.

"Yes, well—uh—thanks," Lacy mumbled, not caring

for the disadvantage at which she found herself. "If you don't mind . . ."

"I said, help yourself!" he repeated curtly, obviously losing interest in the subject. "I can eat whenever it's ready. We'll hold this course for another hour or so on automatic."

He left before she could blunder further and, feeling rather limp, she picked up the cotton suit and escaped, shutting herself in her own closet-sized compartment. Not one of your more comfortable boatmates, she mused as she climbed into the soft cotton trousers and took up the slack about her waist. The fit left a lot to be desired. Jordan was tall, with broad shoulders tapering to a narrow, muscular leanness, whereas she was on the short side and had a tendency to be more rounded than was fashionable. Standing on tiptoe, she studied her reflection ruefully. She had read once that the two things one could never be were too rich or too thin— she struck out on both counts, unfortunately, and in this outfit it showed!

Not feeling particularly venturesome, she settled for steak, baked potatoes, and salad, having first determined that Jordan liked his meat rare.

He would! There was something decidedly carnivorous about him anyway—or perhaps she was just being overly sensitive. Back in Buies Creek, living with Aunt Lottie and seven teachers from Campbell College, Lacy had never run across anyone faintly like Jordan Stone, much less found herself cooped up in close quarters with him. That might have had something to do with the wary expression on her face as she sat across the tiny table from him later.

"Relax," he growled, leaning back after devouring his meal to light a thin, dark cheroot. "You're perfectly safe now." Blowing a stream of aromatic smoke in the direction of the open porthole behind him, he contin-

17

ued rather absently. "I'm glad to see the last of that place myself, frankly. I wouldn't have come in except I needed a part for my vane steerer, not to mention a few fresh vegetables and a case of Belikan."

"I'm awfully glad you did."

He studied her through half-closed eyes, his chair tipped back against what Lacy called a wall and he referred to as a bulkhead. She'd have to watch herself or he'd discover that she didn't know a gimbal from a gooseberry.

"Tell me about Lacy Davis. I take it you weren't traveling alone when you set out. What happened—did the two of you disagree on whether to zip the sleeping bags single or double?"

"It was nothing like that," she bristled, wishing she smoked so at least she'd have something to do with her hands.

"No?" The skepticism in the one drawled word set her teeth on edge and she was tempted to tell him to mind his own business, but in view of the fact that she had more or less made herself his business, she thought better of it. And from the wicked gleam that ignited his eyes, she suspected he knew exactly what she had been thinking.

"My friend was a teacher from my aunt's boarding-house. We were planning to go to Tikal and camp out with a group of her friends who meet there every year, and then we were going to make a side trip to San Pedro for a few days. The Tikal trip was a graduation present from Aunt Lottie—I graduated at the end of the summer session, you see, and then Aunt Lottie's boarders chipped in and added enough for the San Pedro thing so I could see the Caribbean. I've never even seen the Atlantic," she admitted ruefully, completely forgetting her claim to sailing experience.

"So what happened?"

"When we landed in Belize City there was a message from a neighbor of Carolyn's mother. Mrs. Adams had fallen and broken her hip and was in the hospital and Carolyn was needed at home. I should have gone back with her," she said dolefully, "but Carolyn wouldn't hear of it. She said I was to go on to Tikal and she'd get in touch and maybe be able to join us later. Only with the cost of the fare and all, I know she couldn't. And anyway, I won't be there—not at Tikal or San Pedro or—" Her voice wavered suddenly as the full weight of the long day descended on her shoulders. It had been still dark this morning when she had set out from Raleigh–Durham airport, and in the excitement of her first flight she had been unable to sleep a wink on the way. There were all the snacks, and the meals that everyone else seemed to sneer at but had struck her as enormously exciting. And there had been stops along the way, with new people getting on—she had been so keyed up for so very long that now it was as if someone had suddenly pulled the plug, and all her strength drained away. "Anyhow, now," she finished on a sigh, "I don't have any money, or any tickets or anything, and Aunt Lottie saved for years to give me a chance to see something of the world before I settled down to work."

"Cash or traveler's checks?"

"Traveler's checks, but the numbers were in my luggage, so I don't guess I stand a chance of redeeming them." Her eyes were focused on a barometer above Jordan's head and she didn't seem able to tear them away.

He stood up and reached down a bottle from a hanging locker. "I'll get the particulars from you later and see what we can do. Meanwhile, toss this back and hit the hay. The meal was first-rate, by the way, young lady. I'd say you've earned your first night's passage."

He poured her a wineglass of ruby port and served himself something from another bottle. Lacy sipped the sweet wine, found it very much to her taste, and thanked him with a weary smile.

"Glad to find someone who likes the stuff. A friend left it behind and I'd sooner drink cough medicine."

She felt guilty leaving him with the dishes to do but she was out on her feet. It was all she could do to braid the tangled mass of curls and rinse out her mouth with water before falling into the surprisingly comfortable bunk, asleep even as her head touched the pillow.

Sometime during the night a lightweight blanket found its way over her body, but she didn't stir until an unfamiliar motion cut through the layers of consciousness and she opened her eyes to see patterns of light dancing across the overhead paneling.

There was a new toothbrush laid out for her when she stumbled into the head and she splashed off her face and freshened up the best she could with practically nothing to work with. She had washed her hair the night before using soap—she had felt compelled to rid herself of the dust of Belize City—and now it was an untidy mess. If she'd had scissors she would have chopped it off to a more manageable length, but barring that, she used Jordan's comb and rebraided it the best she could.

"Good morning," she greeted, joining Jordan on deck in the iridescent morning mist. "Been up long?"

"Not long. Looks as if the wind's dropped. We'll have to make other arrangements if we're going to keep on schedule."

Startled, she asked, "You mean . . . row?"

He glanced at her to see whether or not she was

joking and then he said, "I think the diesel will handle the job all right. What about a bite of breakfast?"

"How many eggs?" At least she knew her way around the galley by now.

"Make it two, with bacon, toast, juice, and coffee, please. Easy over."

Lacy pushed back the tangles that blew across her face as the braid unraveled itself and muttered something about getting started as soon as she did something with her hair. "I don't suppose you have any scissors, have you?"

Jordan glanced across at her from where he was doing something to the mainsheet winch. The moisture had beaded on his own thick hair and on the strong, angular face. "Why?" he asked.

"Oh, I thought it might be easier to cut it short since I'm going to be sailing for a week or so. I'll never manage to get it untangled without a brush," Lacy answered as she pulled at a particularly stubborn snarl.

Jordan took a clean handkerchief from his pocket and beckoned her over to where he stood braced against the gentle motion of the waves. Turning her back to him, he proceeded to tie her hair back with the rolled-up square of linen. "There, that should do you for a while. Couple of hundred years ago we'd have dipped your pigtail in tar." He grinned. "Now, the next sound you hear will be my stomach growling, wanting to know what happened to breakfast, so scat, will you? Sing out when it's ready and I'll come below."

The day passed in surprising harmony, considering Lacy's state of nervous tension as she watched him at the tiller. From time to time he moved gracefully about the deck doing mysterious things to various ropes, which he called lines and sheets. She lived in fear that he'd ask her to take the helm, but he didn't. He talked

21

idly now and then about various parts of the rigging. She picked up a few terms, even though she hadn't the slightest idea what to do with them.

As the mist burned off, Lacy rolled up her pants legs to take advantage of the sun, and between making coffee, bringing up beer, and fixing snack meals, she listened as Jordan pointed out various places along the coast, telling her what he knew about the area. Late in the afternoon he lowered the anchor in water of an incredible shade of blue. While the *Phoenix* swung idly around with the current, he stretched his powerful-looking arms over his bare shoulders and asked her to fetch him another cold beer and to have one herself.

Lacy made herself a glass of iced tea, never having cultivated a taste for beer. In fact, the sweet homemade wine a neighbor of her aunt's provided them with each fall was about the extent of her drinking.

Jordan pointed out Sepadilla Cay and Placentia Point, little more than smudges on the horizon, as they drifted easily over the slight glassy swells. He eyed her borrowed clothes as he told her about the diving possibilities along the Belize and Quintana Roo coasts. "You'd have to come up with something better than that, though, unless you want to sink fast. The less you wear, the safer you are."

Self-consciously turning down her pants legs several notches, Lacy asked him if they'd be stopping off anywhere along the way. Her tender thighs were beginning to turn pink and she hated to think what would happen to her in anything skimpier, with her perennially pale complexion. She had had little enough time for sunning, having slogged at her books to graduate at the end of the summer session and helped out at home as well.

"Next stop, Isla Mujeres—translation: Island of the Women," Jordan drawled, "and I can already see the fascinating visions your fervid young imagination is conjuring up." His grin was carelessly mocking and it flicked Lacy on the raw for some reason. His attitude had settled into a slightly avuncular disinterest, for the most part, but he seemed to enjoy taunting her about her lack of sophistication.

Her own attitude veered between gratitude and a disturbing physical awareness that she was doing her best to ignore. "It hasn't had time to conjure up anything," she snapped, "but from your tone of voice I gather the name came from something quite ordinary instead of whatever lurid version you expected me to come up with." She did wish he'd give her credit for being an adult, even if a fairly inexperienced one.

"As a matter of fact, there are several stories of how that scrap of land no more than five miles long got its name. One involves pirates and their lady friends and another suggests that when the conquistadores made landfall the island's male population was off on a hunting expedition, leaving only the women behind. Then, too, there are some who say that when Cordoba discovered the place in fifteen seventeen he found a lot of statues of goddesses—stone idols of the female persuasion, at any rate." He flipped the butt of his thin cigar over the side and leaned back, one bronzed arm stretched out along the tiller in seemingly careless control. "None of which has much to do with the woman I'm planning to meet there."

"You're going to meet a woman?" Lacy asked, regretting the question as soon as it was out. It was none of her business if he were going to meet a dozen women. All the same, she couldn't help a small, unreasonable feeling of dismay.

He didn't bother to answer her. Instead, he stood up and scanned the water around them carefully and then announced that he was going to take a dip. "If you'd care to join me, there are probably a few suits in the forward locker. I try to keep a selection on board for guests who come unprepared." The clear blue eyes slid over her speculatively and then he swung himself down through the hatch, leaving Lacy to do as she pleased.

Moments later, catching a glimpse of herself in the more modest of the two bikinis she had found, Lacy wondered who had selected them. The one she wore, a sea-green affair that was little more than three patches held together by beads and ribbons, was preferable to the crocheted thing she had rejected, but her modesty was suffering even before she subjected herself to Jordan's measuring gaze.

It was the labels that made her catch her breath in realization. Jay Stone—Jordan Stone? Was it merely a coincidence? The chain of department stores was well known all over the Southeast, and come to think of it, she seemed to recollect hearing that it had started in New Orleans.

Fancy that! She struck a pose in front of the small stainless-steel mirror—little Lacy Davis of Miss Lottie's boarding establishment in Buies Creek out cruising the Caribbean with a member of the illustrious Stone family. This was better than all her fantasies put together, except for one thing—her view on the relationship between men and women was well formulated, rooted in past experience. She wasn't about to allow herself to forget the pain that could follow a moment's pleasure, not for Jordan Stone or any other macho playboy who happened to be in a position to entertain stray women aboard his luxurious yacht!

"How long does it take to strap yourself into that thing?" he called through the thin door. "Or do you need a hand?"

Without bothering to answer, Lacy opened the door,

brushed past the nearly nude man without a glance, and hastened topside, painfully aware of the raffish grin that followed her. It seemed that in moments of boredom he wasn't averse to entertaining himself by taunting her until she lost what little bit of poise she had acquired.

Chapter Two

Well, let him stare! She might not be in a league with his usual female friends, but she had no reason to hide herself in a burlap bag either!

The water was incredibly silky, surprisingly buoyant, and it was only the question Jordan called out to her from the railing that made her sink momentarily, to come up sputtering seconds later.

"Hey, Lacy, are you as experienced a swimmer as you are a sailor? I'd hate to have to bail you out a second time."

Turning away from the sight of the sun glinting off his bronzed body, she retained an afterimage of the patterns of dark body hair above the narrow band of his white trunks. She struck out in her laborious crawl, learned in the gym pool back at Campbell College. So he hadn't been taken in by her feeble pretensions. He had probably taken one look at her and known she wasn't the outdoorsy type. Exit the sexy tanned blond, surfing with her dream lover in a travelogue sea—enter Miss Lottie's girl, who was more at home in the kitchen than on a ketch!

Still, he hadn't put her on the spot. She'd better be grateful for his casual kindness and stop getting the willies every time he drooped his eyelids in that special way. She could take his teasing, knowing it was only that, for she'd really be in trouble if he decided to put her ashore.

She did a lazy roll and came up smoothly for once, consciously trying to counteract the impression made by that first strangled immersion, in case he was looking. If she had had all the opportunities he had had, then no doubt she, too, would be able to slice through the water in that effortless style he affected. At least she managed to stay afloat!

She swam and dived and then drifted on her back, contrasting her present situation with where she hoped to be in a few short months. She had been lucky enough to get a teaching position in Buies Creek, so that she could stay on with Aunt Lottie, a blessing for them both. It was safe and economical, if not quite as exciting as moving to a strange town, living in her own apartment. That could come later.

"Hey! Time to report to the galley! Unless you were thinking of trying to swim for it. It's a lot further than it looks, believe me, and you wouldn't care for the accommodations if you did reach shore."

She trod water in a circle until she located him floating near the *Phoenix*. The low angled sun shot beneath the hull, making him look as if he were suspended in midair. Lacy still couldn't believe the absolute clarity of the water. While she watched, squinting her eyes against the salt and the sun, he paddled indolently into the shadow of the deep keel, dispelling the illusion.

"Haven't you worked up an appetite yet?"

"Mmmmm, now that you mention it, I think I have." She dog-paddled over to the boarding ladder and laughed nervously as she suffered a sweep from those intensely blue eyes. He was there before she was, holding the ladder, and a current swung her legs against his. To make matters worse, he laughed at her as if he knew exactly how his nearness affected her.

"Up, up, and away," he grunted, placing a hand under her backside and boosting her.

"I can manage by myself!" she protested, scrambling in undignified haste to clutch at the railing and pull herself upright.

"Sure you can," he teased, following her in one lithe movement. They stood dripping on the deck and Jordan picked up a towel—Lacy had forgotten to bring one topside with her. He looped it around her neck and pulled her playfully against his hard, wet body, grinning wickedly down at her indignant expression. "Sure you can, honey—only why deprive a fellow of his fun?"

"I'm not your honey and I'm not here for you to have fun with," she snapped.

"No?" The deep-set eyes narrowed and Lacy shivered as the sun went behind the low bank of clouds on the horizon. "I didn't hear you making any qualifying conditions when you begged me to take you aboard yesterday. In fact, if I remember correctly you said you'd fight tooth and nail if I tried to put you ashore. Changed your mind?"

She was still captive to the loop of towel around her neck, entirely too close to all that muscular masculinity. She could see the moisture glistening on his body hair, feel the heat radiating from him, and she reached out a hand to his shoulder to push herself away when he tightened up the towel.

"What's the matter, honey—afraid I may take undue liberties with your person?"

Her hand slipped on the wet skin of his shoulder and he laughed. "Mr. Stone!"

"Jordan."

"Jordan, then—but please stop doing this—this . . ."

"This?" he queried, holding the towel with one hand while his other brushed the dripping hair from her face.

"No—yes! You know what I mean!"

"You must be referring to *this*," he murmured, the laughter running under his deep voice even as it glinted in his eyes.

By the time the laughter reached his mouth that mouth was touching hers, and she responded with frightening immediacy not only to the personal magnetism of the man, but to the sense of humor that struck a responsive chord inside her.

She could taste the salt on his lips. The sweetness of his flesh was made sweeter by the contrast, just as the heat of his body against hers made the cool breeze on her wet skin feel even cooler. Stubbornly, she refused to open her mouth, and the fact only seemed to amuse him further. Bare flesh against bare flesh, she could feel the laughter shaking his body even while he taunted her lips with his tongue, and then he drew back to smile lazily down at her. "Is that what you're so afraid of, honey? Don't worry—I outgrew little schoolgirls while you were still playing with dolls. In spite of your girlish fears, I think I just may be able to hang on to my self-control until we reach Isla Mujeres."

Much later, after the Caesar salad, the beef Stroganoff, and the kirsch-laced frozen raspberries, Lacy lay in her narrow berth and stared up at the pale reflections above her. Moonlight was dancing across the water, casting out playful patterns that reminded her of laughter.

And laughter reminded her of Jordan and she rolled over restlessly, twisting the borrowed T-shirt under her. He had laughed at her and for a moment she had wanted to laugh with him, but then it suddenly wasn't all that funny. It was condescension at best, rejection at worst, and she didn't care for either one of them. She had napped during the afternoon and now she couldn't sleep. Instead her mind kept throwing up pictures on her mental screen—Jordan as she had first seen him, in faded jeans, a worn cotton knit shirt, and those frustrating sunglasses. Jordan in his brief trunks, poised to go over the side, or sprawled out at the tiller, his dark hair blowing about his head as he squinted against the glare.

Jordan sailing northward to meet some woman—Jordan, who kept a few bathing suits aboard for his female passengers. He had probably never had one before who was embarrassed by the brevity of those suits. She could hear Aunt Lottie's scandalized remarks now if she were to show up at home in any such outfit.

Oddly enough, she wasn't frightened of him—not really. They might as well be two different species. They *were* two different species: one a worldly, wealthy sophisticate who probably had to sweep the women off his doorstep, and the other a meek little mouse who kept her nose to the grindstone and her eyes averted whenever a presentable man loomed on the horizon—and Jordan Stone was presentable! What was infinitely more dangerous, he was likeable. Under all the big bad wolf exterior, she was certain he was an honest, intelligent, caring person. Why else would he have lumbered himself with a useless passenger when he obviously wanted to be alone—or at least with a woman of his own choosing.

What was that woman like? The image that shimmered across Lacy's imagination bore a striking resemblance to the tall, tanned beauty who habitually strolled through her fantasy, her head on the shoulder of a man who was beginning to look suspiciously like Jordan Stone.

Once more Lacy awoke to a pearly morning mist, only today the climbing sun failed to disperse it. By noon the sun was a pale orb playing hide and seek with ragged patches of cloud. A light breeze whipped up waters that had been glassy only yesterday, and the same breeze whipped Jordan's hair wildly about his head as he leaned back, arm extended along the tiller with the jib and mail sheet within easy reach.

Lacy had remained below until some instinct told her she needed a stiff breeze blowing in her face. Now she took her place a little self-consciously on one of the cockpit lockers, pretending an interest in the straining tautness of the sails but terribly conscious of Jordan's extended legs, their contours clearly evident under the damp khaki trousers. He wore no socks, just the soft leather deck shoes, and Lacy, her hands clasped in the kangaroo pocket of her shirt, compared his hard, bronzed skin to her own tender flesh.

Her skin was getting both tenderer and pinker, in spite of the cloud cover. The sun seemed to penetrate even the open-weave cotton of the pajamalike outfit she wore. It was the blue one today; the one she had worn yesterday was rinsed out and flapping disconsolately on the standing rigging.

She made a deliberate effort to shift her mind back to the familiar things she had left behind and would soon return to. About now, she'd have been chopping leftovers into a cream sauce, ready to spoon it into the pastry shells waiting on the counter. Aunt Lottie would be standing in the back door, fussing as her cats fought over the scraps or folding sheets in the laundry room for the seven boarders, all teachers at Campbell College.

In spite of her deliberate efforts to control it, her mind slipped back to the more exciting here and now. Her eyes, even while her mind had been back in Buies Creek, were on those firm, sensuous lips that had kissed her yesterday. That kiss had disturbed her more than she cared to admit. At twenty-two, she had been kissed before, but since she had made it a policy never to date anyone she felt the slightest attraction to, the kisses had been like so much tapioca pudding—pleasant enough, but hardly exciting.

Jordan's kiss, on the other hand, was like nothing she had ever experienced before. It had been a joke, of course—a man who'd been sailing alone for several weeks could be forgiven a distorted sense of humor—but it had been a rather disturbing joke as far as Lacy was concerned, one she didn't care to repeat.

"Jordan, do you often take off like this—by yourself, I mean?"

He attended to a luffing jib before answering her. "I'm no hermit, if that's what you're getting at, and I'm not out to break any endurance records. I guess I just feel the urge to get away every now and then, especially when I have a spot of heavy thinking to do." He flicked her a smile and it ran along her nervous system like chain lightning.

Careful, Lacy—you're not equipped for this sort of thing. "Did you sort it out?"

"Sort what out?"

"Whatever it was that was bothering you." Readjusting her position to ease a cramped leg, she inadvertently leaned close enough to catch a whiff of the mingled aroma of salt, pine-scented soap, and sun-warmed skin that was becoming all too familiar to her. He should

32

bottle it and sell it in his stores as an aphrodisiac after-shave—judging from the effect it had on her, he could make a fortune.

"What makes you think something was bothering me?" He smiled lazily at her, but his eyes were unreadable, squinted against the cool glare.

"You *said* you had some 'heavy thinking' to do," she reminded him, wishing, not for the first time, that he'd treat her as an adult instead of as a troublesome child.

"As a matter of fact, I had a decision to make. Sometimes a lot of thinking can only confuse the issue, so I try to disassociate myself from the problem and forget about it. Then, when I surface again, the answer's all there, written out for me."

Emboldened by his easy manner, she probed further. "And was it there? Have you read it yet?"

"The answer, since you insist on poking your pink-speckled nose into my private affairs, is *yes*. Will that do, or do I have to elaborate?"

"Elaborate," she replied promptly, responding to his air of resigned indulgence with a cheeky grin.

"The answer is yes, I will ask her to marry me. Okay? End of inquisition. Now, how about going below and making a stack of sandwiches and a thermos of coffee. I have an idea things are going to get a lot rougher before they calm down, and you may not be able to do much cooking for the next day or so."

Struggling to grasp the two statements at once, she stood and immediately grabbed for the stanchion as the responsive sloop heeled slightly. He was going to ask her to marry him? Who? The woman who was waiting for him at Isla Mujeres, naturally. What was she like? Beautiful, of course—sexy, intelligent, probably someone from his own social set. A woman who liked to sail—an outdoorsy type, but not a jock.

Standing there at the railing, her eyes staring unseeingly at the turbid water, she wondered why it should come as a surprise—because it had, and not a particularly pleasant one. Which only went to show how silly she was being, for all her degrees and her teaching post! Education and common sense were two different things, and education wasn't going to help her much in this instance.

"Do I have to put it in the form of an order? Hop to it, mate!"

Ducking under the seahood, she dropped down into the galley with only one swift glance overhead. It was distinctly rougher. The scudding clouds were all but snagging on the masthead. "Okay, okay, you don't have to get ornery!" she yelled over her shoulder, and his laughter followed her into the minuscule galley.

Assembling the makings, she began to spread brown bread with Pommery mustard and slabs of corned beef, slices of red onion, and whatever else came to hand. Then she mixed up a container of cheese and olive spread and covered it for later use. Locating two thermos jugs, she made coffee for one and then put together and heated an impromptu bisque to fill the other.

Afterward, she curled up on the wider of the two bunks and tried to concentrate on a book she had taken from the railed-in shelf, but her mind kept straying to the woman Jordan was racing to meet. She recognized the small stab of jealousy for what it was and dealt with it firmly. She had only met the man a couple of days ago, for goodness' sake! Just because they were cooped up here in extraordinarily close confinement—just because he was the first man ever to get under her skin . . .

But that was purely a physical thing. She didn't even know him—not really. It was just a normal biological reaction. After all, her mind might know all about the reasons for her decision to remain uninvolved, but her body didn't. It acted according to its own rules, and unless she wanted a mutiny on her hands, she'd darned well better let it know who was in charge!

There were times when Lacy thought she must have been born with the knowledge of her own conception: the one brief rebellion of a spoiled young girl and the wild boy who had loved her—or so he had said. She knew the date of her parents' marriage and she knew the date of her own birth and there was a discrepancy. But it was only as she became older that she grew to understand that her very existence was at the root of the bitter, hateful quarrels that had been a background to her early life—as much a part of her home as the wallpaper or the rugs on the floor.

Goodness knows there were more than a few of her playmates from broken homes, and they compared notes on their situations because it was a way of life for them. By the time the split became permanent, when Lacy was twelve, she could almost joke about the subject of her parents' most vicious fights.

Almost, but not quite. To know that neither of her parents wanted her, each insisting that the other take full responsibility for the child that had been born seven months too early, the child that had been the only reason for their miserable marriage in the first place, and the shoddy glue that had tried to hold it together—that had been the last painful straw. Lacy had determined silently as she went off to live with an elderly relative she had never even heard of that she'd never marry.

Nor would she ever allow herself to risk having a child that could shape the rest of her life, as she had shaped her parents' lives. That meant, of course, that she must be constantly on her guard against any romantic involvement. Oh, she dated—usually the men who weren't very popular or were too shy to ask other girls out. She told herself that she was doing them a favor, giving them the confidence to go on to greener fields, knowing all along that she was only rationalizing her fears. She ran like a gun-shy bird dog at the approach of any man who might conceivably quicken her pulses.

And now the irony to end all ironies. Her nice, safe vacation—an archaeological trip with a group of middle-aged teachers—had turned into a Caribbean cruise with a man who threatened to make a mockery of all her long-held determination!

Ice melts fast in these latitudes, she reminded herself grimly, and so do good resolutions—and don't you forget it, Lacy Davis!

She put the book away unread and stared at the creased shirt Jordan had flung carelessly across the table. He was a tidy person by nature. Aboard the confines of a thirty-five-foot sloop there wasn't room to be otherwise. Still, the odd shirt, or cigar, or the cap he sometimes wore, tossed aside for the moment, could bring a flush of awareness to her normally pale features. Lucky for her that he would put it down to sunburn!

As the air grew increasingly damp and chilly, Lacy pulled on her sweater over Jordan's shirt and drawstring pants. She had long since discarded her sneakers, finding the smooth rubber soles treacherous on wet decks. The biggest trouble was in getting anything dry once she had rinsed it out. She'd just have to look scruffy—which was nothing new. Maybe he'd come to look on her as a cabin boy, she thought with a wry twist of her expressive mouth.

They had sandwiches for lunch and then, under Jordan's strict supervision, Lacy took the helm for a brief, exhilarating turn. She could feel the vessel lunging under her hand as if it were alive, feel the vibrations of every wave as it lifted them and then passed beneath them. About the middle of the afternoon, she helped Jordan douse the sails and watched as he started up the auxiliary engine.

"We'll have to make the best time we can during daylight hours and lay over at night," he told her, moving agilely past her to do something to the tiller. She watched avidly, eager to learn, excited by the Winslow Homer seascape all around her, fascinated to a dangerous degree by the man who was everywhere at once.

"Just tell me what to do," she called against the increasing whine of the wind, "and I'll do it!"

He grinned at her after the wind carried his words away. A few moments later he stopped long enough to throw a companionable arm around her shoulders and press her briefly against his side. "That's the way I like my women," he teased. "Sweet tempered, quiet, and obedient."

"Pick any one of the three and consider yourself fortunate," she jeered, liking the feel of his wiry strength braced against the wind. Liking the look of him, too, she acknowledged silently as she stole a glimpse at his strong features. He was staring out across the water, although they had long since lost sight of shore, and the last of the teasing warmth was soon replaced by a frown. "These aren't the best waters for nighttime navigation under the best of circumstances. If only I weren't in such a hurry, it wouldn't matter so much, but . . ."

He broke off and went below and she heard the static and squeals from the marine radio on the teakwood console. After several minutes he called up to where she stood in the hatch. "Well—you heard the man. A tropical storm!"

Lacy, whose ears couldn't separate and interpret the

distorted sounds that came from the bank of meaningless dials and gadgets, moved to stand beside him. Tropical storms to her were circular diagrams on a weather map after the six o'clock news. "Are we going to run into it?"

"It's hanging offshore between Cuba and the Yucatán Peninsula with every possibility of turning into a full-scale hurricane. November," he swore impatiently. "When's the last time we had a hurricane in November?"

The question was rhetorical and Lacy remained silent, watching the eerie glow of the instrument lights as they highlighted Jordan's frowning features in the growing gloom. It was steamy down here now, and she lurched past him to go to her compartment and exchange the sweater for one of her borrowed shirts. If things got much rougher she'd be afraid to move about at all. As it was, she had a rapidly darkening bruise on her shoulder from the last time she had tried to use the head.

After his initial outburst of impatience, Jordan kept his worries to himself, but Lacy was aware of the deepening furrows between his thick, dark eyebrows. He seemed to make a deliberate effort to iron them out as they finished another meal, complimenting her on the soup. She told him modestly that it was only a combination of canned tomato and pea soups with a can of small shrimp and a good-sized dollop of some sherry she had found in the hanging locker. "The stuff may taste like medicine, but it does add something extra to the soup, doesn't it?" She gazed at him smilingly, unconsciously begging for his approval.

"It should," he remarked dryly, "considering the quality of the blend." He didn't elaborate and Lacy, deflated, didn't inquire. If she had used the wrong thing, then she was sorry, but it was too late now, and besides, Jordan's mind had already turned to something more serious than a cup of wine.

There was little conversation for the next hour or so before it became too dark to see at all. Jordan's attention was taken up with charts and channel markers and the radio crackled continually. Finally he must have located the landmarks he was seeking because he altered the course to steer directly for the low, scrubby landmass that he told her was the lower tip of the Mexican state of Quintana Roo. With the quiet hum of the electric winch he lowered the anchor into waters that were relatively protected by a jutting finger of land.

"We'll lay over here until first light and then, if at all possible, we'll up anchor and head north again. We're too damned exposed here on this shore. At least if we can make Isla Mujeres, or even Cozumel, we'll have the protection of a harbor of sorts." He showed her their position on the chart and the position of the storm, which was still only a tropical storm but was hanging stubbornly in the same area, refusing to move on.

The next two days were an unending time of holding on to whatever was at hand and taking advantage of momentary lulls in the sickening motion of the boat to make coffee by the gallon and whatever cold meals she could manage. If Jordan slept, Lacy was unaware of the fact. After a while she began to mark the passage of time by the darkening of his beard. His eyes became dulled and reddened and seemed to recede even deeper under the prominent shelf of his brow, and his voice, when he spoke to her, was clipped and distracted. She might have been just one more of the convenient appliances he depended on. Push a button, coffee is produced; push another and a sandwich comes forth. The only thing that might attract his attention, she thought perversely, was if the machine failed to produce on command. It must be some woman who could keep him going in the face of a probable hurricane. Perhaps she should suggest that he radio his proposal if it was all that urgent. It seemed once the mighty Jordan Stone got around to making his mind up, neither rain nor snow nor threat of hurricane could keep the lover from his appointed rendezvous.

As time stretched on unendingly, however, Lacy forgot Jordan and his soon-to-be fiancée. Three things impinged increasingly on her consciousness: the continuous wailing dirge of wind in the rigging, the stuffy breathlessness of the enclosed space below decks, and the growing uncertainty of her stomach. She tried fixing her eyes on something steady, but there was nothing steady in her world, so she tried closing them, but that only made her more aware of the relentless motion— the elevator lift, the breathless hovering, the plunge and wallow and then . . . the whole cycle beginning all over.

She tried breath control and found it worked better than anything else, but as the hours grew into days and the days into all the time there was, she felt increasingly awful and her mind seemed to plod along with but a single thought—get me back to shore!

Sometimes Jordan talked, but he might well have been talking to himself. He remained topside most of the time, but now and then he'd erupt into the steamy, unbearable little world below, his yellow foul-weather gear streaming water that was half rain, half seas, and he'd wolf down a sandwich from the covered plate and mutter under his breath as he whirled dials and messed about with charts to the tune of the deafening crackle of static, code, whistles and whines, and the odd, disembodied voices.

"The blasted thing's stalled in the middle of the

Gulf," he growled through a bite of corned beef and mustard on pumpernickel. "At least we've cleared Banco Chinchorro. If she's still hanging on by the time we make Punto Herrero Light, we'll wait it out in Carranzo Bay. I hate like the devil to waste the time, but . . ."

Switching off the cacophony, Jordan reached for his dripping foul-weather gear and turned to look directly at her for the first time since coming below. "How're you doing, honey? Holding up all right?"

Lacy only prayed she didn't look as green as she felt. Swallowing a fresh surge of nausea, she managed to smile weakly and nod, but she might as well not have bothered. He had already turned away, taking the steps three in a single stride and latching the hatch behind him.

Chapter Three

At last there came a day when the sun shone, weak and watery, once more. Jordan had come below sometime before daylight for food and drink and had helped himself to the last of the sandwiches and the coffee that remained in the thermos, which was probably luke-warm by now.

Lacy hadn't been able to summon up the energy to make some fresh, even when the gale dropped and Jordan was able to hold the *Phoenix* into the wind, making the going relatively smooth. In fact, it seemed days since she had managed to do much more than get up off her knees in the cramped head, but with the coming of light also came an easing off of the nightmare motion that had left her drained, both figuratively and literally.

"Lacy!" he yelled out now.

From her berth Lacy swallowed and attempted a normal-sounding answer, but the voice that emerged was weak and raspy-sounding against a throat that was raw from hours of dry heaving.

He appeared in the doorway, filling it completely. "What the devil!—are you seasick?" he barked, tugging at the neck of the faded blue pullover he wore under the yellow slicker.

The very word was enough to trigger another wave of nausea and she moaned and rolled over to face the wall. At the moment she felt better than she had in ages, but she still felt perfectly horrible. She wished he'd go away and leave her to live or die in peace—at the moment she didn't much care which.

"How long have you been this way?" he demanded, sliding a cool hand across her forehead.

"A month . . . a year."

"When's the last time you ate anything?"

"Don't be obscene," she groaned, attempting to dislodge the hand that lingered on her head.

"Good lord, honey, why didn't you tell me?"

She didn't even bother to answer that. He had had his hands full without feeling obligated to play nursemaid to an unwanted passenger—not that there was anything he or anyone else could do other than transport her magically to dry land.

Eyes closed, she sensed his absence and the suffering descended on her full-fledged once more, bringing with it the curious knowledge that for a moment it *had* lifted.

Before she could make up her mind whether to kneel before the throne again he was back, levering her up from the pillow with a surprisingly gentle hand. "Here, sip this—small sips now, don't gulp it."

He held the Coke for her and rather than protest she obeyed him, allowing the liquid to trickle down her abused throat. After several sips he muttered something about dry crackers and then he pulled her forward against his chest while he thumped up her pillows. "They'll be pretty limp, but pack 'em in anyway. Get as many down as you can and I'll be back in a minute with a dose that'll put you back on your feet in no time."

He left her then and it was as if the remaining strength she possessed seeped through the pores of her skin, leaving her empty and shaken. By the time he reappeared, looking tough and big and concerned, she was gazing at the space he had left with far more longing than she knew, and for a minute he studied her face from the doorway. Then, as if a cloud had passed over the sun, his eyes became opaque and he dropped down beside her, holding two small tablets and a glass of water.

"Swallow 'em both, turn over onto your left side, and sleep."

Sometime later Lacy cautiously opened her eyes again. She felt almost human. Had it been a day—two days? She couldn't remember the last time she had eaten, except for the cola and crackers, and her knees felt like boiled spaghetti. Before she could even reach the door, Jordan was there.

"Decided to rejoin the living? Good. Go splash off your face and climb into a bathing suit. Stage Two of the Stone treatment coming up."

"Don't use that phrase," she groaned, and he grinned at her, looking disgustingly magnificent in a three-day growth of beard.

When she emerged some fifteen minutes later, Jordan had peeled down to the minimal bathing trunks he favored. He subjected her to a leisurely scrutiny, taking in the sleep-tousled hair she had hastily braided and the too-pale face, its only color a pair of oversized gray-green eyes and a pink and peeling nose. For once she was glad she tended toward the plump side; she had certainly shed a few pounds—the hard way.

Registering neither approval nor disapproval, he said, "We're going to swim for a few minutes to clear the fog from your system and then, while you rinse off and climb into something dry, I'll put together a meal out of whatever we have left."

Lacy cast a doubtful glance at the choppy waters. The aquamarine clarity had given way to a sort of milkiness, but the color was still spectacularly beautiful. "Are you sure you recommend swimming as a cure for—you know?"

"Hair of the dog," Jordan pointed out gravely. Then his lips twisted in a crooked grin and he told her they were just inside Carranza Bay, where it was considerably calmer. "Next stop—Cozumel." He crossed his fingers and flipped them under her chin. "Now, over you go."

She still had her doubts. It would be awfully nice just now to sprawl out on the sun-warmed deck and bake her bones. For once she tended to favor the line of least resistance.

As if reading her mind, Jordan said, "Most refreshing thing in the world when you've been cooped up too long in a stuffy cabin. It'll get the circulation going again, and then, after I feed you, you can go up forward and doze in the sun—put a little color back while I cruise on up toward our next landfall." His hand cupped around her neck in a casual gesture and she caught herself wanting to hold it there. "Hurricane Jeanne's finally moved on, dumping a flood of rain on the mainland, but other than that behaving herself pretty much like a lady."

"My first hurricane," Lacy mused aloud. "My first dose of seasickness, too," she added with a grimace.

"Don't let it put you off small-boat sailing, honey. It's not everyone's cup of tea, but you know, I think you might take to it, in spite of a rough inauguration."

"Oh, don't worry—now that it's behind me, I'm kind of excited about the whole thing. I figure things can only get better from now on."

His smile was indulgent, slightly teasing. "So you think you've seen the worst, do you? Well, I guess I'd better see to it that you have smooth sailing from now on, hmmm?"

Suddenly embarrassed lest he think she was angling for an invitation to prolong the trip, she took a header over the rail and swam underwater until she had to come up for air. That was the trouble with dealing with a man of Jordan's age and experience—she couldn't tell when he was joking and when he was not.

He must have followed her over the side, but he swam around her lazily, not making a point of watching her, but making her feel safe nevertheless. For all his occasional brusqueness, he could be amazingly tactful.

"Time's up. Come on now—let Uncle Jordan heave you back on board."

"I told you—stop using those horrid terms." This time she could answer his grin with one of her own and she paddled over the the boarding ladder and allowed him to steady her as she found her footing. It was only her imagination that made it seem as if his hands lingered on her waist, slid slowly down her hips as she climbed the narrow structure. Cursing the thin complexion that revealed every nuance of emotion by a rush of blood, she hoped if he noticed the increased color he'd put it down to the five minutes of sun she had soaked up while floating around in the bay.

Stop acting like a silly, overimaginative schoolgirl, she rebuked herself a few minutes later as she allowed Jordan to towel her unraveling braid. He had pulled her to him, leaning the top of her head against his chest as he gave the dripping, tangled mop a final rub. She had showered off, as per his instructions, hurrying back up on deck as soon as she'd wriggled herself into one of the baggy pants suits.

"I thought you might put on the other bikini and get a bit more sun."

When she refused to comment, he chuckled. "I told you, honey, you don't need to be afraid I'll lose control. Don't forget, I'm about to get myself engaged, which is supposed to confer some sort of immunity, I believe."

Grasping at a subject to hold up between them like a shield until she could develop an immunity of her own, Lacy asked brightly, "Tell me about her. What's her name and what does she look like?"

They were sprawled out on the deck, enjoying the slight breeze that diluted the sun's heat, and Lacy bit into the thick sandwich Jordan had provided to go with the hot, milky tea. It seemed to be a combination of everything available and she only hoped her stomach wouldn't protest.

"Her name is Lolene MacArthur, and she's tall, lean, blond, and beautiful."

"Naturally." She sounded exactly like Lacy's dream self—the antithesis of short, rounded, freckled, and curly haired. "How old is she?"

He shot her a withering look. "Old enough to be interesting, at any rate."

"Meaning I'm not."

He grinned, and it took some of the sting out of his words. "Meaning you're more of an irritation than a fascination," he told her, and when she would have swatted him, he ducked away, laughing openly. "Sorry, honey, but you were asking for it. Anyhow, you wouldn't want to fascinate an old roué like me, would you? You probably have the boys back at school tied up in knots—or is there one special one waiting for you to see the world and hurry home to him?"

"No special one," she replied airily. "I play the field."

His laughter was mildly irritating, but she ignored it. So all right—he could laugh at her silly pretensions. What would he think if she told him that the only field she had ever played was the one behind Aunt Lottie's, where she and Avery Clodfelter had made up Frisbee games to play with his dog?

"I do wish you'd stop treating me as if I were fourteen."

He reached over and placed his empty beer bottle where it wouldn't roll overboard and turned to her again. "So you're a big girl, all graduated from school and ready to tackle the real world. Maybe I should have listened more closely when you told me about yourself. It seems I've been underestimating you."

"Don't patronize me! I may not be as well traveled or as experienced as you are, but frankly, I wouldn't swap places with one of your sort for any amount of money. And if you think that's just a case of sour grapes, then that only goes to show how cynical and dissolute you really are under all that phony charm!"

"Whoa—enough, kitten! Maybe I'm just trying to figure out how to deal with a sweet, unsophisticated small-town girl. Did you ever consider that?"

"Not for a minute," she snapped skeptically. "You don't have to 'deal' with me, as you call it."

"All the same, with your vacation plans on the rocks, I'd hate to have you go back home disappointed." His tone was facetious, but then he turned and reached an arm across her waist, tugging her closer.

"I don't need that sort of thing, thanks!"

"No?" he drawled, the taunting gleam of his eyes partly hidden under lazily lowered lids. "Well, according to your own words, you're a big girl now, so I'd say that makes you fair game, wouldn't you?"

Her teeth were practically chattering as her heart thumped crazily under the thin cotton shirt. Where was that fine protective edge of disdain? "Don't forget about Lolene," she threw out as a last-ditch effort to stave off the touch that her traitorous body was already craving.

"Forget Lolene." His hand was warm on her waist, and he closed the space between them and propped himself up on one elbow so that he was looking down on her.

"You don't sound much in love, considering that you're hurrying to ask her to marry you." She could feel his breath stirring the unruly tendrils that the salt air curled around her face.

"Don't I?" One of his fingers traced the short span of her nose, and the Venus hollow below it before moving on to her mouth. His words sounded almost detached. "Let's just say I stopped sending Valentines a long, long time ago, and since then I've never professed to anything more than a healthy degree of lust."

Calling on every vestige of resistance at her command, Lacy twisted her head away from his feathery touch, away from those mocking blue eyes. "Then why on earth are you asking her to marry you? Does the poor woman know what she's letting herself in for?"

"Oh, I think we can safely assume that Lolene knows precisely what she's getting. If the arrangement doesn't suit her, then she's perfectly free to say so, with no bones broken on either side."

Wincing at the callous attitude, Lacy considered the irony of finding herself arguing the case for a marriage based on mutual love—or marriage of any sort, for that matter. She stared stubbornly up at the masthead fly, but her peripheral vision took in entirely too much of the darkly mocking face beside her. Every cell in her body was aware of his nearness, like a flesh-and-blood radar system, pinging out frantic alarms.

"Suppose we leave the affairs of my alleged heart to me, hmmm?" The words were spoken against her shoulder, and then Jordan's lips trailed to the base of her throat.

Still she tried to swim against the overwhelming currents. "In other words, mind my own business," she snapped, her voice sounding unnaturally strained.

For an answer Jordan pinned her arms out on each side of her, lowering his face to within an inch of hers. "I warned you. Maybe you should have stayed a little girl," he muttered, and then his lips touched hers with surprising gentleness, brushing across them softly before settling into place.

She kept her mouth clamped firmly shut, and then she felt him begin to laugh. Completely disconcerted, she allowed her resistance to falter for just a second, but that was all it took. He twisted her mouth so that her lips parted, and then he invaded, and there was no more room for anger, for indignation, or any other emotion except the overwhelming sensuous languor that stole over her. Her hands fluttered ineffectually to his shoulders to push him away, and then lingered to draw him closer as her deliquescent bones lost all strength to resist.

One of his hands moved aimlessly under her shirt, caressing her side, the shallow valley of her midriff, before moving to find her breast. When incredibly delicate fingers feathered lightly around the sensitive nipple, she moaned against his mouth.

The sun was a sullen orange globe hovering just above a low-lying bank of lavender clouds, and the deeper water had turned to purple against the turquoise shallows. Neither of the two people lying entangled on the deck of the sloop noticed. Jordan's long, muscular limbs were bronze under a light covering of hair, and his back glistened damply as Lacy's small pale hands traced sleek, hard muscles from their source along his spine. When he raised himself enough to tug the loose shirt over her head, allowing the sun one quick glimpse of milk-white breasts before covering her torso with his own, she sighed heavily and abandoned herself to a reckless, mindless sort of urgency.

Her eyes remained tightly closed, shutting out everything but the feel of his lips, his hands, his body; nevertheless, she was acutely aware, as if her skin had eyes, of his gaze devouring her body. With infinite gentleness he lowered his lips to touch the proud peak of each breast, and she caught her breath in a shuddering little gasp. When his hands moved to the drawstring of her pants, however, she caught at them with her own, twisting her head from side to side.

"No, Jordan—please, no," she whispered. "I don't want this."

He was perfectly still for a moment and she dared not look at him. She knew very well he had every reason to despise her for leading him on and then stopping short, but she couldn't help it. Something inside her—the internal gyroscope that had held her on course since the first stirrings of adolescence—would not let her go on.

"I'll let you off easy—this time. You've just been through the mill. But Lacy—a word of advice. Don't try that trick too often." His voice was harshly flat, and she cringed from its lack of emotion.

How could she tell him—how could she explain why she couldn't risk engaging in casual sex, no matter how fashionable it had become in her age group? Especially when she had gone along so eagerly up to a point. "Jordan, you don't understand—I can't explain, but . . ."

"Forget it," he said harshly. "The last thing I want now is a dose of true confessions!"

Stung, she reached for a weapon. "What about Lolene? I should think you owed her a little more loyalty," she said with a quiet dignity that came from somewhere outside herself.

He leaned over and tossed her her shirt. "Cover yourself," he rasped, but when her hands fumbled the job, it was Jordan who pulled out the inverted sleeves and shoved her arms through the proper holes. "Not that it's any of your business, but I'm still a free agent."

"And always will be," she retorted angrily, "wife or no wife! Well, I can tell you this much, Jordan Stone—"

"Spare me, please! I can do without a lesson in morality from some green—"

"Not all that green," she blurted mendaciously. "Just because I don't care to make myself available to some—some playboy with the morals of a tomcat doesn't mean I'm inexperienced! It just means I happen to have learned a few lessons that you've obviously missed!"

He applauded slowly, sarcastically. "A touching performance, my dear. Letter perfect, too, but then if you trot it out every time some man turns you on it's no wonder."

"You don't think you're the first man to do that, do you?" she challenged rashly.

He lifted his eyebrows in a weary lack of interest. "Hardly. And now, if you don't mind, I'll leave you to your righteous indignation."

She glared after his retreating form, hating the turbulence inside her and hating him for making her feel this way. "I hope Lolene has the good sense to turn you down flat!" she called after him. "And what's more, I hope it hurts like the very devil!"

By the time Jordan came alongside the concrete quay

reaching out from the little town of San Miguel on Cozumel, they were speaking again, but barely. Lacy had cooked the meals, taking her own up forward to eat alone as she stared out morosely over the incredibly beautiful scenery.

She was seated on the bow, her legs dangling over the side, when Jordan sought her out after making fast between two weathered but gaily decorated tour boats.

"Finished sulking?" he asked blandly.

Without turning around she said evenly, "I'm not sulking. There's just nothing at all we have to discuss."

"Not even a trip ashore, with dinner thrown in for good measure?"

"I'm not hungry," she retorted, still without turning around. "If I do go ashore, it will only be to find someone else to give me a lift stateside."

She could actually feel the quick anger radiating out from him, striking her back with the ferocity of the noonday sun. "You set one foot on shore without me and you'll find yourself in over your stupid little head! You haven't seen trouble until you tackle the Mexican immigration authorities! Don't forget one thing, girl— you're here illegally, and you'll have to do one whale of a job convincing them that you're innocent! Believe me, they cut their teeth on kids like you, out to make a fast buck with a bit of free enterprise!"

Gripping the rail until her knuckles whitened, Lacy wondered where the greatest danger lay—in throwing herself on the mercy of the authorities, or in remaining with a man who, without even trying, could make her toss out every hard-won principle with hardly a fight. "And I suppose you'd thumb your nose at them! Really, Mr. Stone. I'm amazed you even bother with a boat. Why don't you just *walk* to Isla Mujeres?"

If the sound of his receding footsteps was anything to go by, Jordan Stone was angry—extremely angry—

and Lacy, when she heard those footsteps leap lightly across to the pier and fade away, remained where she was, staring ferociously at a pelican that flapped laboriously past a few feet above the glittering surface of the water. Her back was turned to the town, and she waited all of ten minutes to see if Jordan was coming back before she drew in her legs and twisted around to stare dismally at the colorful little group of buildings.

There seemed to be plenty of activity ashore. Too early yet for dinner, it was nevertheless late enough for couples and small groups to be wandering up and down the waterfront gazing in shop windows, slowing to check out an occasional restaurant, and stopping every few yards to talk. A stocky young man with a rifle over his shoulder went past on a silent little motorcycle, carrying an iguana by the tail. Something for the dinner table, no doubt.

Probably some of the tourists were North American. Possibly some of them were here on their own yachts—there were several palatial ones anchored around in the small harbor. Surely one of them would be willing to take on an unscheduled passenger who could work her passage home in the galley, if not in the rigging.

The whole time her mind was parading out reasons for seeking another means of transport, another part—an undisciplined part that had been born within the past few days—was shaking its head in silent rejection. Her rebellious alter ego stubbornly insisted on her remaining as close as she could for as long as she could to the man who had the ability to turn her bones into liquid fire with a single touch.

Heaving a baffled sigh, Lacy unfolded herself and stood up, wondering if Jordan would be back for his dinner or if he had had enough of his ungrateful passenger. She couldn't blame him. She supposed she had been throwing out mixed signals, but all the same, he had no business taking advantage of having her more or less captive. There ought to be some sort of rule governing the behavior of an experienced man with an inexperienced woman in these circumstances.

Leaning over the rail to gaze down into the glassy still water, she pondered the strange dichotomy that had taken control of her lately. She had always been so levelheaded, so sure of where she was going! She could have sworn she'd be proof against this sort of temptation, but then she'd never before been exposed to such a heady mixture—the tropics and Jordan. Jordan alone was enough to undermine the most determined creature, if that creature happened to be female. And Lacy was only now coming to realize just how very female she was!

Her troublesome thoughts accompanied her below decks, where she foraged in the refrigerator for the cheese and olive spread she had made before the storm. It was only an infatuation, but it was her first, if one didn't count the crush she had had on Avery all those years ago. Ridiculous at twenty-two, but then she had been extremely careful not to expose herself to temptation. She hadn't had the time, what with school and working for her aunt, but that had been all a part of the master plan, too. And now—it was rather like measles in someone who had never been exposed before; it could do considerable damage if one didn't take precautions.

Jordan didn't return until quite late. Lacy, feeling alternately angry and sorry for herself, had long since gone to bed, if not to sleep. Used to the more soothing sounds at sea, she found herself resenting the bursts of laughter, the music, and the snatches of conversation that drifted in and out of range, sometimes in English, more often in Spanish.

There was no warning of Jordan's arrival until the

hull lurched under the burden of his weight. Her heart reacted immediately to a surge of adrenaline.

"Lacy? Are you awake?" he called softly through her door.

She stiffened, clamping her eyes shut against the light that filtered through the porthole from the nearby town. She heard the door open and felt his presence as he moved silently to stand beside her berth.

"Quit playing games, Lacy."

Her eyes flew open and she glared up at him. Even from where she lay she caught a faint whiff of the pine soap he favored, the expensive cheroots, and the tang of rum. "Get out of my room," she ordered coldly.

He was carrying a paper bag as he pushed her legs toward the backside of the bunk and sat down beside her. "I brought you a peace offering, honey. Don't you want to see it? I thought all women liked presents." His long legs almost reached the opposite wall. She felt suffocated. He took up far too much space in the cramped compartment.

"You're drunk!"

"Not really. Just a little something to steady my nerves," he admitted mildly.

She glared at him. "If they were any steadier, you'd be immobile! Now, would you mind leaving so that I can go back to sleep?" she demanded with exaggerated patience.

"You weren't asleep, Lacy," he said softly, running a finger from her knee down to her ankle and then stroking the sole of her foot through the light covering of the sheet.

"Certainly I was!"

"No, you weren't. In the first place, you were too riled up to go to sleep, and I'll lay odds you waited up to see when I'd come back, in what condition, and with whom. Am I right?"

She remained grimly silent.

"Well, my little sea waif, I hate to disappoint you, but I'm all alone, without so much as a long blond hair on my lapel—if I had a lapel, or a smear of lipstick on my collar—if I had a collar."

He was wearing his usual khakis with a sun-bleached black knit shirt, and even in the near darkness she could see him quite clearly. His strong teeth gleamed in a wicked smile that made her blood boil. "Just a shot or two of the old devil rum. So what do you think of that, sweetheart? Haven't I been an exemplary fellow?"

"What do you want from me, a medal for good conduct?" Her scathing tone was lost in his burst of laughter and she caught her breath. "Jordan, leave me alone or let me go! I don't care which, but I refuse to stay here and let you—and be a—" Her voice broke and she tried to twist away, but he was too quick for her. He leaned over, bracing one arm on the other side of her, and his hand was warm against her stomach.

"What—or who—are you so frightened of, Lacy? It must be yourself, because I told you I wasn't interested in green girls, didn't I?"

"You said—you said you outgrew little schoolgirls while I was playing with dolls," she told him, her voice faintly accusing, "but that you thought you could last out until you got to Isla Mujeres."

She tried to ignore the feel of his body heat, so close to her. "You evidently didn't count on being so—so bored that you'd settle for whatever was at hand." Her sarcasm came out sounding disconcertingly like self-pity, which only made her angrier.

"Ahhh, so you remembered my exact words, did you? I didn't realize what a profound impression I had made on you—I'll have to watch those little pearls of wisdom, or I'll be having to answer to you for every careless word."

He was teasing her, mocking her vulnerability, and she shut her eyes tightly against the sudden sting of bitter tears. "I wouldn't believe you, Jordan Stone, if you told me the sun rose in the east! Your views on things like honor and integrity—if you even know the meaning of the words—are miles apart from mine! I only hope Lolene can survive being married to a man who's totally selfish and completely without morals!"

He was silent for so long she cringed. Finally she stole a look at him, at the sharply etched profile against the pale paneling of the bulkhead. At the bleakness she saw there she opened her mouth to take back her charges. She hadn't really meant them—she was only fighting against what was happening to her with whatever flimsy weapons she could find. "Jordan," she blurted.

"Forget it, honey. I'm not sure Lo will appreciate your concern for her well-being, but don't take it to heart. Try and get some sleep, hmmm? There's something I want to show you on the way up the coast."

His hand slid up over her waist as he stood, picking up the paper bag absently. Before he straightened up he shook her shoulder gently. "Maybe before you go back to Buies Creek you can pass on a few of those worthy lessons you've learned, unless you think it's too late to try and reform me."

Chapter Four

By the time Lacy opened her eyes again they were at sea. She felt the lift of the bow, heard the snapping and creaking that told her they were under sail, and by the time she had dressed and poked her head outside, the sun was halfway up the mast, making strong shadows of jib against main.

"Morning, Lacy," Jordan called out, just as if he hadn't gone out drinking last night and come back to undermine her newly constructed defenses. Anger wasn't going to do the job for her—it was hard to remain angry when she liked him so much. She ventured a smile, and he smiled back at her, saying, "We're wung out and on our way to the Island of Women."

"We're what?" she crowed, moving out to join him in the cockpit.

"Wung out. Jib to starboard, main to port, catching

every bit of wind while we're running. Watch yourself, honey—can't have you swept overboard by a gibing boom just when you're beginning to have such a salutary influence on me."

One glance at the laughter dancing in those mocking eyes was enough for her. She ducked back inside, muttering something about breakfast. It remained to be seen just who was influencing whom, and at the moment she didn't feel up to delving into the matter. One thing about it—a head full of high-flown theories didn't amount to a drop in the ocean when it came to actual practice. It was a good thing he'd be back among his own kind soon, with Lolene ready and willing to take over his entertainment. There'd be no more trouble along those lines once he set his sights on his tall, slender, sexy blond. By this time tomorrow he'd probably already have shoved a diamond the size of a hubcap on her third finger, left hand.

"Make it three eggs this morning, honey," Jordan called out from the stern, where he was leaning back beside the tiller soaking up raw sunshine like a khaki clad pagan god. "Half a dozen slices of bacon, too, hmmm? About a quart of coffee ought to do it."

It was a good thing he had sacrificed an extra berth for additional food storage with an appetite like his, she thought irritably. Blast him, he didn't even have the grace to be hung over!

They had been out little more than an hour when Jordan pointed the sturdy little sloop up into the wind and doused the sails. "Let's take a break. In case you don't make it back to the neighborhood anytime soon I want to show you something special," he remarked, moving lithely to drop both anchors in waters of incredible clarity. "Go climb into a bathing suit—how about trying the crocheted one this time?" he suggested wickedly. "You're making me think you don't like my taste in bikinis."

"Don't hold your breath," Lacy retorted, feeling an unaccountable surge of elation for no good reason at all. Diving below, she dug out the skimpy string bikini and held it up consideringly before discarding it in favor of the more modest one. "Don't be an utter idiot, Lacy. It's rough enough without that!"

Just *what* was rough enough she didn't dwell on as she struggled to tie the cords behind her neck without entangling them in her hair. If they were going to remain in these latitudes much longer, she'd simply have to do something about it. What had been a sheaf of thick, but well-behaved wavy brown hair back home in North Carolina had now become a wild, unruly mass of sun-streaked curls here in the damp salt atmosphere.

Padding barefooted to where Jordan waited, she braced herself against the raw sensory assault of that bronzed, muscular perfection in the extremely brief white trunks. The sun had turned his moderate coating of dark body hair into rich gold and she fought down a desire to run her fingers through it. Instead she leaned against the rail to peer down into the crystalline water.

"Ever done any snorkeling, Lacy?" Jordan held up a mask and fins.

"Nope. Not since I tried breathing through a straw lying on the bottom of a creekbed with a rock on my stomach to hold me down. That was about fifteen years ago."

"Intrepid adventurer, aren't you?" he teased, leaning over to swish sea water over the masks.

"I thought it was pretty good under the circumstances," she declared airily. "I wasn't the champion, though. Avery Clodfelter, the man in my life at that time, won hands down using a section of hosepipe and making his brother sit on his chest until his mother found us and hauled us all out of the creek. The boys were grounded for two weeks and Mrs. Clodfelter wouldn't let me play with them anymore, but Avery said that I wasn't half bad—for a girl."

While she struggled to get the mask fitted properly without pulling her hair too badly, she was aware of Jordan's lazy, if thorough, scrutiny. When his eyes finally lifted to the level of hers again, he grinned openly at the flush on her cheeks. "Tell Avery Clodfelter he has a very discerning eye," he taunted softly.

Her indignation didn't last. It was no match at all for the sparkling brilliance of the day and the fact that, to her chagrin, she *liked* the man! Aside from being so painfully, dangerously vulnerable to his powerful physical appeal, she had to go and like him!

"Ready?" he asked as they stood poised to go over the side. "Follow my lead until you get your bearings, will you?" He took her hand and they jumped feet first into the tepid waters.

For half an hour or more Lacy explored a fantasy world of delicately colored forests, with castles and sea gardens peopled by unbelievably brilliant fishes, from tiny darting flashes of color to curious, lethargic creatures who approached her outstretched hand with a complete lack of fear. There were purple ones, rosy reds, greens and golds, and any number of patterns and combinations, and she wished she knew the names of at least a few. They seemed to drift along through the slanting shafts of sunlight, through waving branches of fan coral and the statuesque staghorn, like a corps of exotic ballet dancers, turning in unison at some silent signal to drift in another direction.

Jordan caught at her shoulder when she surfaced, allowing his hand to slide down to her wrist as he led her back to the *Phoenix*. She had just discovered the trick of diving and then clearing her snorkel and she hated to leave the fascinating reef so soon, but she obediently tugged the mouthpiece from her lips and slid her mask up, waving her feet in the clumsy flippers. Her legs were already beginning to ache with the unaccustomed exertion as she reached for the boarding ladder.

"Had enough of Palancar Reef?" he asked with an indulgent grin.

"I'd never get enough! Jordan, it's incredible! How can I ever thank you for showing it to me?"

The smile started in his eyes and then spread to his wide, expressive lips, and Lacy flinched inwardly at the knowledge that soon she'd be seeing the last of that rugged face with its startlingly blue eyes and the crooked grin.

"My pleasure, sweetheart. Think you can haul yourself back on board, or shall I give you a leg up?"

Thinking of those hands lingering on her bare body, Lacy shook her head and reached for the supports. She might not make the most graceful job of it, but she'd prefer to manage under her own steam.

It was hot as Jordan raised the anchors, and Lacy sought a place in the shade to drink her iced tea. Instead of hoisting the sails again, he started up the auxiliary, and she watched through half-closed eyes as he tipped back his head to down the last of his beer. Muscles worked smoothly under the gleaming tanned skin and then he wiped his mouth with the back of his hand and tossed her the empty can. "Stow that for me, will you, girl?"

She missed the catch and had to roll over to reach it and the deck burned her bare skin. Neither of them had bothered to change, being satisfied to get something cold and refreshing to drink as they resumed their course to Isla Mujeres. Besides, Lacy didn't have all that much to change into. She had washed out her own things again, but they'd still be damp when they reached their destination. As hot as it was in the sun, the humidity was fierce, and she rather thought the salt air had something to do with the fact that nothing dried as rapidly as she would have expected.

She was still toying with the idea of finding herself some other means of transport once they reached Isla Mujeres when she went below to organize something for lunch. The fresh vegetables weren't all that fresh by now, but she mixed them together with some canned garbanzos and a couple of hard-boiled eggs. Grating cheese over the mixture, she dressed it with an herbed oil and vinegar and took Jordan's out to him, along with another beer. The few he drank each day seemed to have no effect on him.

She watched him from her place in the shade, seeing the way his features became almost grave when he forgot her existence. Something seemed to be bothering him, but she didn't care to risk a snub by asking.

The uncomfortable thought occurred to her that it might be her own presence. Could Jordan be courting trouble with the authorities by harboring—what was she, an illegal alien? Perhaps she had been watching too may thrillers, but there was definitely a problem over her papers—or the lack of them—and she'd hate like anything for Jordan to wind up in hot water on her account. Maybe it would simplify things for him if she just slipped away quietly once they got to the island.

Lying on her stomach on the bow, her legs stretched out beside the forward cabin, Lacy watched the sun turn the western sky into a rose, green, and gold panorama as the smudge of Cancún grew larger on the horizon. Jordan had told her that the beach development there was only a few years old, having been conceived as a totally planned resort community containing everything a larger city could boast. At the moment there were only half a dozen or so hotels to be seen from this distance, their white sides catching the gilding glow of the setting sun.

There were ruins at nearby Coba, presently undergoing exploration, according to Jordan, but his mind was obviously on something other than Mayan ruins at the moment. The closer they came to Isla Mujeres, the more morose he grew.

Shortly after passing off Cancún they veered away from the mainland, and as they neared their island destination Lacy had the strangest feeling that she was existing between the covers of a travel magazine. Although the sun had already disappeared beneath the water, its ambience touched everything with shades of gold and copper. The water beneath them changed constantly from ultramarine to turquoise and then back again as they moved silently over the sandy bottom with its random patches of turtle grass. According to the charts down below, the maximum depth was about thirty feet between the island and the mainland.

As they neared the harbor, passing close to what appeared to be an altar on a rock in the middle of the channel, Lacy began to pick out the variety of boats assembled along the waterfront, wondering which one was carrying Lolene MacArthur. There was an enormous fleet of sturdy-looking trawlers at one end of the anchorage, and closer to the small town several gray naval vessels.

They rounded a red buoy near a red-and-white-striped lighthouse that nestled cozily among a fringe of palm trees and cruised surprisingly close to the shore.

Lacy continued to study the scattering of yachts. They couldn't compete with the small, colorful native fishing boats, with their turquoise and cobalt, red, and gold decorations, to her way of thinking. The small craft hauled up along the white shore, with their beautiful and often whimsical trim, bore the same stamp of individuality that set the *Phoenix* apart. Only now was she coming to appreciate the style and gracefulness of Jordan's sloop, with its custom-built white hull and the black and teak trim.

Her gaze moved slowly among the larger yachts. Somewhere out there, possibly within hailing distance, was Jordan's Lolene. Was she watching them approach? What would she think when she saw Lacy aboard the *Phoenix?*

Stirring herself reluctantly, Lacy turned to watch as Jordan skillfully maneuvered the sloop into mooring position. He had selected a place slightly apart from the others. About fifty feet away was a rather tattered-looking ketch with an assemblage of bathing suits and towels flying like pennants from the rigging, but by far the most impressive yacht in sight was an enormous vessel that looked as if it might be a junior member of the Princess Line. There was even a helicopter perched up on top of its hotellike superstructure. Surely *that* wouldn't be the MacArthur yacht!

She studied Jordan's face for a clue, but if he were excited, he hid it well. If anything, he looked slightly grim as he calmly went about the business of coiling lines and securing the sloop. She should probably be helping, but for some reason a sort of apathy had settled over her—a sense of anticlimax. Besides, she'd do better to remain out of sight until he explained her to his fiancée, after which it might be a good idea if she were all ready to leave.

Not that she had any idea of how or where or when. But later, when Jordan came to find her, she was seated on her bunk dressed in the white jeans and her dark red sweater.

"What's the idea?" he asked, bracing a hand against the open door as he surveyed her from the top of her braided hair to the tips of her stained sneakers.

"The idea of what?" She felt inexplicably defensive.

He moved into the cramped quarters to toss a paper bag down beside her. "The idea of getting yourself gussied up in all your worldly possessions and sitting down here like a refugee waiting for a sponsor."

"Is there any good reason why I shouldn't wear my own clothes?" she asked with stubborn logic.

"I thought you might feel a little more comfortable in this." He nodded to the parcel beside her. "That sweater can't be too comfortable in weather like this."

A little warily, she opened the bag bearing the logo of a boutique on Cozumel and took out a stunning embroidered blouse in white cotton gauze, a pair of white shorts, and a gathered skirt in a handsome handwoven pattern of navy and turquoise. She lifted an accusing face to him. "You have no business buying me clothes."

He swore in exasperation. "Spare me your small-town inhibitions, please! Look, there's no point in your feeling conspicuous when we join Lo and Tad and the MacArthur clan."

Distracted momentarily, she asked who the various members of the clan were.

"Tad's Lolene's brother—a few years older than you are. Since they were planning on making the trip in the *Lobell III*, I assume that means Horace, plus his third wife, and half a dozen or so hangers on."

"What will you tell them—about me, I mean?"

He lifted his shoulders and let them fall again, and in spite of her searching gaze she could read nothing of his thoughts. His control, when he cared to exercise it, was almost total. "What's wrong with telling them the truth?"

"Nothing. I'd really prefer it as long as you don't think it will upset your—Lolene. But she might kick up less of a ruckus if she thought I'd only hitched a ride from, say, Cozumel, instead of sailing with you all this time."

The air inside the tiny cabin was stifling and Lacy tucked her feet under her as she moved back against the bulkhead. There was hardly room for one, much less someone else of Jordan's size. It wasn't his actual physical presence that disturbed her, though. He might pretend to be calm and collected about the imminent meeting with Lolene, but she had an idea he was more disturbed than he'd have her think—probably over the presence of his uninvited female passenger.

"I'll tell her how I threw myself on your mercy if you'd like me to," she offered diffidently. "And you can explain that I'm going home just as soon as we can straighten out the mess about my papers."

Slicing through the air with an impatient gesture, Jordan told her to forget the idea of taking off the minute she got a chance. "I told you I'd get you home and I will, but in my own time! I have enough on my mind without having to worry about you taking off and getting yourself in trouble again."

Angrily, she came to her feet in a single movement and found herself practically on top of the irritating man who seemed to have taken over her life. She stepped back and there was nowhere to go, for he moved with her, his hands coming up to bite into her shoulders. She flung back her head and glared at him, trying to maintain her anger in the face of something alien that seemed to be creeping into her bloodstream.

"I wouldn't blame her for refusing you if you turn up to propose to her with me hanging on to your coat-tails," she jeered. "What if she turns you down? Will I get the blame for it or can your overweening masculine pride take a rejection in its stride?" She was courting disaster. Some irrational force was making her throw out challenges she hardly understood herself, and she saw quite clearly by the flame in his eyes the instant he accepted the challenge.

"You're asking for it, aren't you?" he said softly, boring into gray-green eyes that suddenly darkened with panic. Instinctively, she twisted away, but he was too fast for her. He caught her chin and held it with bruising strength while he lowered his face to hers, staring mockingly into her eyes until the last possible moment.

By the time he lowered her to the bunk, Lacy found her resistance had melted away like mist in the sun. By turns aggressive and seductive, Jordan reduced her to the point where she was holding his head, clinging to him openly while he teased her with tiny nibbling kisses on her eyelids, her nose, the corners of her mouth. He had pushed up her sweater at first and then, with an impatient oath, had held her off the bed and slipped it over her head, leaving her in only her jeans and a scrap of lacy bra. If he had decided to remove those too, she knew with a sinking fatalism, she would not have prevented him.

"We shouldn't be doing this—not now of all times," she whispered into his thick, warm hair. He was stroking the rise of her breast with a tantalizing tongue, causing her breath to flutter shallowly in her lungs. Her voice was merely a catch in her throat.

"No?" he mused, pausing in his depredations to unclip the band of her bra. "A little late to be thinking of that, isn't it?"

He captured the dusky rose nub with his lips and began to torment her as his hands invaded the waistband of her jeans. When she heard the metallic sound of a zipper, she bolted upright in alarm and Jordan rolled to one side, propping his head on one hand to survey her lazily. She could see quite clearly the driving pulse in his throat, but when he spoke his voice revealed only the slightest trace of unsteadiness. "Any more challenges you'd care to toss out?" he dared her.

She cut her eyes at him in distress. "I didn't!"

"Don't hand me that," he said derisively. "I can disprove it in a minute and we both know it."

Lacy reached for her woolly sweater and Jordan caught her hand. He took out the white blouse with its navy, turquoise, and coral embroidery and put it in her hand, closing her fist around the material. "Wear this. I'd hate to have to nurse you through a heat stroke from your pure cussedness."

"Get out then," she surrendered grudgingly.

He obliged, casting her one more warning over his shoulder as he went. "I'll do the talking. You just smile sweetly and say your party piece if and when I call on you. Got it?"

"Yes, *sir!*"

He grinned infuriatingly and closed the door after him.

On deck, Lacy joined him at the rail. There were probably three dozen boats of all sizes within hailing distance, not counting the navy vessels and the shrimping fleet further into the cul-de-sac of the harbor. The afterglow of the sunset was bathing them all in an apricot warmth and Lacy thought that if there were a perfect way to see an island in the Caribbean for the first time, this was it. She inhaled deeply, attempting to sort out the exotic scents that assailed her nostrils. "Which one is it?" she asked softly, not wanting to disturb the peace of the moment.

Beside her, Jordan shook his head slowly. "I'm afraid we've missed them. Either that or . . ."

Her heart thumped and seemed to swell in her breast and she forced herself to stare intently at a segment of orange peel that floated gently past. Don't let her be here, don't let her be waiting, she uttered silently, and then added in disgust, What good would that do you, you silly little fool? He's a man with a man's inclination to take what's offered and never look back. Do you want to follow in your own mother's footsteps, for goodness' sake?

In a voice curt with impatience Jordan spoke. "Morningstar!"

Lacy looked at him questioningly, but he had forgotten her presence for all the attention he paid her. She followed his glance to where a gleaming white launch was setting out from the largest yacht in the harbor, the one with the helicopter perched on top.

It took only a very few minutes for it to reach them and in that time Lacy was able to study the woman who stood in the bow, her flowing dress fluttering in the breeze. It could only be Lolene. Tall, sophisticated—who but a woman of infinite assurance would dare to wear white chiffon to paddle about between boats in? Her hair was the color of narcissus, more white than yellow, and her face was perfection. From the bottom of her heart Lacy envied her those cheekbones and that flawless complexion.

"Hallo, darling," the woman called out as soon as they were within reach of her voice. The voice, too, was perfect—husky with just the right amount of drawl. "I didn't think a little thing like a hurricane would keep you away. What've you brought along? A mascot?"

Jordan caught the painter and fastened it to a cleat before holding out a hand to the blond Texan.

"Oh, no, you're coming with me. You know I can't abide these little boats. Come on, we're ready for drinks and I missed out on my first just to come escort you back to the *Star*," Lolene invited.

Jordan remained where he was and Lacy, wishing herself anywhere else, hadn't the nerve to simply walk away.

"You came with Morningstar?" Jordan's voice was hard with some element Lacy found impossible to interpret.

"Oh, Daddy started in on Tad again and one thing led to another. We decided to come along with Naylor instead. I suppose sooner or later Daddy and Daphne will come chugging after us." She looked pointedly at Lacy, her eyes narrowed under lashes that were patently false. There was a measuring look in those pale, cool eyes that Lacy, for all her discomfort, couldn't blame her for. She started to speak and Jordan laid a deceptively casual arm across her shoulders, his hands biting into her bones with a quelling force.

"Lolene MacArthur, Lacy Davis," he murmured, then, nodding to the helmsman, he returned his attention to Lolene and told her that he and Lacy would be across in half an hour or so. "Meanwhile, have your drinks. Lacy and I can catch up later on."

"But Jordan . . ." the blonde protested, but Jordan nodded once more to the young man at the controls of the Boston Whaler and the protest was lost in the loud roar of the engine.

As they veered away, leaving the *Phoenix* rocking in the wake, Lacy thought she'd hate to be in the young crewman's shoes once that noisy engine quieted down, for she had an idea Lolene MacArthur was extremely capable of expressing her displeasure.

Chapter Five

"Who or what is the Morningstar?" Lacy asked softly once the sloop had settled down again. Jordan was staring after the launch as it sidled up to the floating dock beside the yacht.

At first she thought he hadn't heard her and she decided to allow discretion to be the better part of valor and pretend she had never asked. She studied him covertly, admiring the shape of his nose and the way his thick hair sprung from his well-defined brow. It was impossible to discern his mood and she wasn't at all certain she wanted to. He seemed to be bothered about something and that something had to do with his girl friend—which meant that he wasn't at all pleased to see Lolene here with Morningstar, whoever Morningstar happened to be.

As if hearing her thoughts instead of her earlier words, Jordan spoke, still staring out to where the enormous boat lay at mooring like a giant floating hotel. "Naylor Morningstar is probably the biggest pirate south of the Mason–Dixon line," he said softly, with a chilly lack of emphasis.

It was almost an hour later when Jordan and Lacy crossed the several hundred feet of glassy water to the *Morningstar II*. Jordan had changed into whites after showering and had remained in his cabin until Lacy had just about decided he wasn't planning to join the others for drinks and dinner. She had removed her jeans and put on the skirt in some half-conscious reaction to the sight of Lolene, resplendent in white chiffon, but to her consternation she realized she had nothing to wear on her feet except for the tennis shoes, and they looked ludicrous with her new finery.

Jordan, after one swift look that took in her new blouse, the white jeans and, unbeknownst to her, the look of strained anxiety on her face, asked why the jeans.

In reply she extended one small foot. He frowned in immediate understanding and she marveled at the fact that he should care, under the circumstances. It couldn't matter all that much to him that the stray he had collected along the way would be more than a little bit uncomfortable among the other guests wearing her none-too-clean pants. Hand washing in cold water wasn't very effective when it came to getting out real grime.

"I don't suppose you'd consider letting me stay here?" she ventured hopefully.

"Sorry. We'll stay up front with this thing all the way—otherwise your reputation will be so much confetti before the night's over."

Thus she found herself accepting a steadying hand from an attractive man of some fifty years or so. He introduced himself as Naylor Morningstar even as his slightly pouched eyes were covering every inch of her.

"Well, well, well, what have we here?" he speculated rather unoriginally, turning to greet Jordan. "And I wondered at this penchant of yours for solitary sailing," he jibed. "Come along to the bar—we've been at it since the sun crossed the yardarm and it's under the keel by now."

There were some dozen or so of them in all, plus an equal complement of crew in starched tropical whites to serve drinks and hors d'oeuvres. The men were dressed more or less alike in white pants, with either white or dark shirts, some ruffled and some starkly plain. The women wore anything from white chiffon to black evening pajamas, and Lacy felt conspicuous in her jeans. The jewelry ranged from elegant to barbaric, but the least of it cost more than she spent in a year on herself.

"I'm Tad," a thin, rather clever-looking young man announced. "You've met my sister and I'm dying to hear how you managed to snag Jordan. For an inside story I might even try to fend off Lolene's poison arrows." He grinned conspiratorially and Lacy discovered she didn't care for him very much in spite of the fact that he was the only one who had volunteered any conversation at all—if you could call it conversation.

Remembering Jordan's decision to stick to the truth, she told him very briefly how she came to be aboard the *Phoenix*. "So your sister can save her ammunition," she added. "I'm only along until Jordan can straighten out the mess with my papers and funds—then it's back home to Carolina."

Tad MacArthur had just launched in on a slightly malicious rundown of the guest list when Jordan appeared at Lacy's side. "Sorry to break up your fun, but if you're as hungry as I am, Lacy, you'd better not linger." He took her arm and steered her away, leaning over to speak softly in her ear once they were clear. "Keep away from him. He's trouble."

Irritated at his proprietorial attitude, Lacy pulled away and glared at him. "That's not a very nice thing to say about your future brother-in-law. I thought he was very friendly."

"So's a piranha," he retorted dryly.

Dinner was far from comfortable, at least as far as Lacy was concerned. There were half a dozen courses of beautifully prepared and flawlessly served food, but her appetite seemed to have fled. All around her the conversation seemed to consist largely of gossip, from behind-the-scenes shoptalk to outright character assassination. It was all done in a clever, entertaining way and Lacy began to feel as if she had stumbled into a sophisticated play. Surely real people didn't chatter amiably about someone's sabotaging a cartel out of pure spite or trading a hotel for someone else's favorite mistress.

She toyed with the lemon shrub—sherbet floating in champagne and garnished with lemon slices—and decided she didn't need anything more in the alcoholic line. There had been wine with every course plus a fruit mixture marinated in liqueur, and not even the fresh breeze that was filtering through the palatial dining room could erase the dizziness that was beginning to assail her.

After dinner there was music on the afterdeck and several couples began dancing. Lacy sought a secluded place to hide in until she decided whether or not to be sick. She watched the dancers, breathed deeply, and after a while decided she'd live. Then Jordan danced past with Lolene clinging to him like a limpet, her airy chiffon tangling in his long, muscular legs, and she decided maybe she wouldn't.

"So, we find the charming little stowaway playing hide and seek," Naylor said from behind her.

Lacy craned her neck as he leaned over her, his arms draped on each side of her head across the back of the deck chair. "Hello, Mr. Morningstar. Not a stowaway —not really. You see . . ."

"Spare me, darling—it's enough that he's brought you here. I'm beginning to find Texas platinum a little overpolished. Perhaps I've been overlooking the charming qualities of Carolina agate."

He might as well have completed the simile with scrap metal, Lacy thought, undecided whether to be amused or outraged. At least he didn't pretend she was anything other than a common mineral—not even one of the semiprecious stones that abounded in North Carolina!

"Thank you—I think."

He came around beside her and dragged up another chair. Settling himself, he leaned forward confidingly and took one of her hands in his. "Lacy . . . lovely name, child. Tell me all about yourself. For instance, how did you really get mixed up with that odd character and his toy boat?"

His fingers were tracing patterns on the palm of her hand and Lacy barely managed to suppress a shudder as she eased her hand away on the pretext of smoothing her hair.

"I was going to Tikal with a teacher friend of mine, but when we got to Belize City, Carolyn—my friend— got a message and had to go back home. You see, her mother . . ."

Naylor interrupted her impatiently. "Oh, all right— if that's the story, you must stick to it. I must say, it's romantic—the bit about the papers and your traveler's checks adds the finishing touch. Well thought out, all in all, but then you've had plenty of time to work on it. How long did you say the two of you were together?" His eyes, large, watery brown ones set in a welter of wrinkles, bored through her and Lacy felt her temper begin to rise rapidly.

"Mr. Morningstar," she began irritably, when Jordan appeared before her and held out a hand.

"Lacy? Ready to head back to the *Phoenix?*"

There was nothing at all in his expression to indicate he was displeased; all the same, Lacy felt suddenly, quite certain that Jordan was seething like a volcano. Meekly she allowed him to pull her up from the chair over Naylor's protests, and when he bid a rather terse goodnight and thanks for the hospitality to their host, she smiled her own thanks rather uncertainly and followed along behind him.

Lolene was nowhere in evidence and Tad was wrapped around a pretty redhead whose name was Jenny Something-or-other and so they left the yacht with little or no attention, to her relief. It had occurred to her during the course of the evening that Lolene might not want her to remain aboard the sloop with Jordan and the only alternative that suggested itself immediately was unpalatable—that she move aboard the larger yacht and allow Lolene her room on board the *Phoenix*.

Neither of them spoke on the brief voyage across the harbor. Lacy swung over the side and took the painter from Jordan as he tossed the seat cushions under the cowling, out of the way of a sudden shower or a heavy dew, and then he came aboard and took it from her. She had watched admiringly on many occasions as he threw a knot he called a bowline into a line with a deft flick of a wrist. Tonight he broke all previous records for speed in securing the dinghy and Lacy, afraid his lightninglike actions were indicative of his temper, disappeared below before he had finished securing for the night.

The next morning she awoke feeling stuffy and headachy. Part of that was due to the alcohol she had consumed the night before, no doubt, but part was due to the fact that it had rained during the night—one of those sudden, unexpected showers that blew in from the Caribbean. Jordan had obviously come in to close her porthole and her room was stuffy. The very fact that he had entered while she was sleeping made her feel . . . vulnerable somehow, although reason told her he had had little choice if she weren't to be soaked to the skin. He had probably not even cast her a glance.

She drew her knees up and hugged them as she picked randomly over the events of the previous night. So *that* was the woman Jordan had decided to marry. He could have done far better. Looks and money weren't everything, after all, and he probably had more than enough money—as well as looks—for both of them.

Oh, and you wouldn't have a personal interest in his affairs, would you, Lacy A. Davis? Hoping he'd take one look at that blond paragon and turn to you with a cry of discovery?

Fat chance! The Jordan Stones of this world didn't bother with the Lacy Davises except for the odd fling when nothing better presented itself. When it came to marriage, Money married Money, Family married Family—which left a certain little would-be school-teacher completely out of the running. Stack up Lolene's stunning looks, her platinum-plated background, and her sophistication beside Lacy's assets and what happened? Looks? Lacy's wild mop of unruly curls and a perpetually peeling nose fell far short of sophistication. Money? She was starting from so far behind she'd never catch up.

She sighed heavily and reached over her head to open the porthole. That left Family. That left *nothing*, as far as she was concerned. She wasn't illegitimate—at least her name was her own—but the knowledge that she was born early and unwanted—that had followed her all through her life, and if she ever needed to heed the inherent lesson, it was now.

Now that she had all but fallen in love with a man who wasn't above taking his pleasure where he found it. He was like her own father in that, she supposed, if in nothing else. Only in her case a marriage was out of the question. Jordan had never pretended to offer her anything more than mutual satisfaction—on a purely temporary basis. He had told her from the beginning that he was going to marry someone else, nor did he pretend to care for her—or for Lolene either, come to that. His heart—his alleged heart, as he called it—wasn't involved. Jordan didn't believe in love. He'd be ruled by his head in all matters and no head that contained a particle of sense would incline him in her own direction—not when the alternative was Lolene MacArthur.

So—enough of this breast-beating! Two aspirins, a shower, and a bite of breakfast, and then she'd see about getting on with the business of securing her release. Surely there'd be a tourist bureau on Isla Mujeres. If she had a tourist card, then perhaps Jordan would be able to lend her the money for a ticket home if they couldn't make good her lost traveler's checks.

All sorts of promising things to look forward to, she

told herself brightly, but when she climbed out of her narrow bunk and headed for the shower her feet dragged lethargically and her eyes were cloudy.

Once more she found herself aboard the *Morningstar,* or the *Star,* as she was familiarly called—this time for lunch with those guests who were awake by one thirty in the afternoon. At least this time she was more or less dressed for the occasion, for Jordan had taken her ashore, and after making arrangements to have her birth certificate and several other papers sent to nearby Cancún by Air Express, they had gone to the bank, where he had dealt efficiently with the matter of her lost checks.

No one in the bank spoke English—in fact, she discovered that few people on the whole island spoke English, and the majority of the tourists were from other countries—but Jordan coped admirably, handing over an incredible amount in pesos. She had to take his word for the currency exchange, for without sitting down for a session with a calculator she was more or less helpless.

She bought shoes first and then, at Jordan's suggestion, a dress in a stylish batik and another set of underwear. Her most prized possession, however, when they got back to the sloop she was coming to think of as home, was a hairbrush. It was gaudy, plastic, and absurdly expensive, as was everything on the island, but when there was a captive audience, what else could one expect?

For lunch aboard the *Star* she wore her skirt and blouse with the white macrame sandals and she felt almost attractive with her hair brushed into its best behavior and anchored on top of her head—until she peered closer into the stainless steel mirror and grimaced at the sight of a pink nose, with a fresh crop of freckles straying across her cheeks.

From the moment they stepped on board Jordan was claimed by Lolene, leaving Lacy to fend for herself until Tad came outside and discovered her. His narrow face brightened immediately and he crossed the carpeted afterdeck to greet her, ignoring the redheaded Jenny, who called to him from one of the deck chairs.

"Peel down and let's take a dip before lunch," he suggested.

"I didn't bring my bathing suit." Now that she noticed it, most of the others wore only the briefest of suits with a jacket over it—which meant she was still odd man out.

"Jenny'll lend you one," Tad offered, signaling the younger girl and making his demand before Lacy could prevent him.

Jenny, whose last name turned out to be Wainwright, seemed willing enough, and since the others, including Jordan, were wandering over to a small swimming pool, she went along reluctantly.

"Leave your things here," Jenny told her, indicating the sumptuous cabin they had entered. She dug out a selection of some half a dozen suits and Lacy chose a brown jersey one piece, asking if it would be all right.

"Be my guest," the other girl said airily. "Naylor has scads of them if you don't see anything here you want. Lo would probably lend you one, too—or maybe she wouldn't," she added quizzically. "What's the real scoop with you and Jordan? When y'all dropped anchor last night and Lo saw the pair of you on the *Phoenix,* she practically had a fit."

"But we explained," Lacy began, folding her blouse and skirt neatly and laying them over the chair.

"Oh, sure, that bit about finding you down and out

somewhere in the boonies. But I mean, really—how'd you meet up with him and convince him to bring you along? Jordan's been Lo's property ever since they cut their teeth on the same playpen. Their daddies had a store together, you know. That was the first one, and when they split up—only the business, not the families —why, Jordan and his Dad started up another one and another until Jay Stone had spread all over the South, just like mushrooms. Want a cap or do you mind getting your hair wet? Lordy, I wish mine would curl that way!"

"No cap," Lacy laughed, "and I'll trade you any day of the week. Yours is lovely!" In fact, she decided with the warmth that comes from recognizing a friendly spirit, Jenny was really far lovelier than the more sophisticated Lolene.

Swimming in a small pool on board a yacht was a totally new experience. It would have never occurred to her that a yacht could afford the space, but when a yacht was the size of the *Star*, it could afford space for whatever whim its owner had. She had already learned of the billiards room below and a small projection room where first-run movies were screened nightly.

"I prefer Venustiano Carranzo or Palancar Reef, don't you?" Jordan said from a few inches behind her.

Lacy, startled, tried to turn around, bumped into someone, and submerged, and Jordan lifted her by a handful of her curly wet hair, laughing down into her face as she sputtered to get her breath. "I wish you wouldn't startle me that way," she panted. They had moved to the deep end of the pool somehow and she was forced to cling to Jordan's forearm while she regained her balance.

"We're stuck for lunch but let's duck out of here afterward. I want to show you something of the island if you're interested."

"Of course I'm interested!"

Gliding smoothly up alongside them, Lolene, looking golden in a white maillot, asked. "Interested in what—or need I ask?"

"Interested in doing the tourist bit, Lo. Would you like to take in the local sights?" Jordan answered composedly. At Lolene's appearance Lacy had tried to disengage herself from Jordan, but he captured her elbows and held her afloat in front of him while he engaged in a conversation with his girl friend.

It was agreed that they'd make up a small party that afternoon to cycle to the southern end of the island to view its only ruin. Then Lolene claimed Jordan's attention for herself as she brought up the subject of her father's running quarrel with Tad, a subject that was evidently well known to both of them.

Lunch was slightly more comfortable than dinner the previous night had been, thanks largely to Jenny's friendliness. It was when Lacy headed back to the cabin to put on her dry clothes that she ran into Lolene.

"Spare me a minute, Lacy, " Lolene more or less ordered, holding open the door to a stateroom that made Jenny's comfortable quarters look like a pantry.

Warily, Lacy crossed the white furlike carpet and accepted the edge of a pale green velvet chair. She waited for the older woman to speak.

"I understand your papers will be in order by tomorrow at the latest. Jordan was planning to sail you across to Cancún and have immigration there fix you up, but I've come up with a better solution. I can have Gus, our helipilot, fly you over and get you settled aboard a flight in the morning. That way you won't have to impose on poor Jordan any longer."

"Oh, but—"

"You'll admit he's been more than generous with you."

Lacy blinked uncertainly. "Well, of course, I . . . he arranged with the bank for my checks to be redeemed, and . . ."

"Don't be so naïve! Jordan gave you the money from his pocket. You're not stupid enough to think all you have to do is walk into a bank and ask for a certain amount of money, with no proof, no receipt or anything! Or are you?"

With a sickening lurch, Lacy's brain ran headlong into what had been bothering her ever since their easy negotiations. Jordan hadn't even had to present them with the name of the firm issuing the traveler's checks! He had simply strode up to the window, turned on that rapid-fire Spanish of his, and walked out counting pesos. The paper she had seen exchanged must have been one of his own bills!

"Yes, well . . . it was a loan," she explained a little desperately. "Jordan knows I'll pay him back as soon as—"

"Spare me the details, honey. You've already reimbursed him, no doubt, and don't think for one minute that it bothers me. After all, Jordan's a *man*, if you know what I mean, and I'm certain you do, but fun time's over now. It's time for you to trot on back to wherever you came from and let him get back to his own kind."

"I'm not stopping him as far as I can see," Lacy managed coldly. "I've wanted nothing more than to go home, but it hasn't been possible up until now." She was still in her wet bathing suit and with the air conditioner turned on full blast she found herself sitting rigidly upright, trembling from a combination of nerves, temperature, and temper.

"There'll be a room tonight at the hotel for you— Posada Del Mar. I'll have Gus come for you in the launch early in the morning. Meanwhile, enjoy your day of sight-seeing. It must be exciting for someone like you to find herself vacationing on a Caribbean island."

Of all the condescending . . . *witches!* Lacy did her best to assume a dutiful meekness. "Yes, ma'am. Thank you." She stood, sensing the interview was at an end, and at the door she glanced over her shoulder to see the older woman reclining on the chaise longue, a chiffon and maribou negligee tossed over her bathing suit and a lazily satisfied expression on her beautiful face.

On the way back to the *Phoenix* Lacy held her tongue. If Jordan questioned her tight-lipped silence, he kept it to himself. When she boarded the sloop she went directly to her room and began scrambling in the trash can for the receipts that had come with the clothes Jordan had bought her. When she finally found them, they were all in pesos and she couldn't decipher them, much less interpret them. She had seen enough to know that everything here on the island was terribly expensive. She had probably already overspent the amount she had set aside for shopping in the first place and now, with the possibility that she wouldn't be able to make good her checks . . .

Oh, it was hopeless! Of all people to be indebted to! It was enough that she had almost lost her senses over the man—an infatuation was bad enough—but to owe him money was the final blow! She had at least counted on being able to pay her way home!

She could hear drawers slamming in his room a few feet away. For all its close quarters, she much preferred the *Phoenix* to the plush *Star*. If one were going to be on a *boat*, then one should *feel* as if one were on a boat!

She gathered up her few belongings and began to fold them into one of the recovered paper bags. Not the batik. He might be able to get his money back for that, at least. Nor had she worn the shorts. Oh, bother! Why hadn't she settled for a trip to the Asheboro Zoo instead of trying for a once-in-a-lifetime experience? She'd managed to lose her luggage, her purse, her heart, and her reason—all within a matter of days—and now the only thing she had left, her pride, was sinking without a trace!

Jordan tapped on her door and opened it without waiting for an answer. He looked around and his eyes came back to her with a clear question. "What's the occasion?"

"I'm packing to move into the hotel," she answered impatiently, glaring down at the sweater she was folding. It wasn't his fault she had to go and make such a fool of herself!

"The devil you are! What put that idea in your mind? Is that pile of pesos burning a hole in your pocket or aren't my lowly accommodations good enough for you now that you've experienced the luxury aboard the *Morningstar?*"

"Jordan! You know better than that!"

"All right, so I know better. Then tell me what you're moving out for? Doesn't the view suit you?"

She sighed and laid the sweater down on her bunk. "I thought it was probably your idea in the first place. Didn't you suggest to your girl friend that I'd be better off tonight in a hotel?"

"Whatever gave you that idea?" He came inside and the room shrank alarmingly.

She didn't bother to reply. It wasn't needed, but when Jordan's brows lowered threateningly, she took a deep breath and tackled him on the other matter. "About my traveler's checks, Jordan . . ."

"You're not going to any hotel! Forget that idea," he interrupted.

"About my traveler's checks," she insisted, looking him in the eye now.

To her astonishment, a dull flush crept up under his rich tan. "Forget the checks. You're all squared away now, aren't you? If you need any more, I'll be glad to lend it to you."

She didn't know whether to cry or to slug him! Instead of doing either she turned away and her shoulders heaved in a big sigh. She seemed to be doing a lot of that lately. Jordan covered her shoulders with his large hands and turned her to face him and she stared at the place where his body hair curled over his collarbone. She could even see the slow, strong pulse that beat there just under the skin.

"Lacy—has someone said something to you?"

A broken laugh escaped her and her eyes lifted to his derisively. "Don't tell me you're suffering from a guilty conscience!"

"All right, so I jumped the gun a little on a few things. It's not important, is it? We've got your documents coming in tomorrow and once we get you all legal and accounted for, we'll explore a few of the other islands in these parts. How does that sound to you? We could even go—"

"Jordan," she pleaded. "Stop trying to evade the issue! You gave me money—loads of it—and told me it was mine. Why couldn't you have simply told me it would take a while to get my checks reissued?"

"It's all the same in the long run. I just thought it was simpler this way, that's all. After all, I'm the one who has to look at you across the table day after day and the view's improved considerably since you stopped parading around in my clothes." His grin invited her to share his amusement, but she was determined not to allow him to get out of it that easily.

"Listen to me, Jordan," she commenced.

"Hush," he whispered, lifting a finger to her lips. "You argue too much."

"Jordan, we're going to have this out because by tomorrow I'll be . . ."

"If I can't shut you up one way, I can another," he warned her, and before she had time to evade him, he had lowered his head to hers.

This time she didn't even pretend to resist. Her mind might clash with his high-handed way of doing things, her words might duel with his whenever they tried to come to terms with matters between them, but when his mouth claimed hers and his hands brought her body up so close that she could feel his every muscle straining closer to her, she was lost. Whatever sorcery he used on her, she couldn't fight against it, and the pathetic thing was she didn't even want to!

"Hmmmm, you taste like honey and almonds," he murmured against her throat. He had to lean over her and it seemed only natural to equalize the difference between them by lying down—it happened with or without her own cooperation, she had learned. Then he was crowding her against the bulkhead on the narrow bunk, laughing into her neck in that sensitive area just below her ear.

She gave one last try for sanity. "Jordan, you shouldn't be doing this."

He whispered huskily in her ear so that a tremor raced violently through her body. "Shall I tell you what I'd rather be doing?" He ran his hands up along her ribcage, lifting the gauze blouse free of her waistband, and she allowed him to pull it over her head.

This was madness—utter, irresponsible madness! While his lips tugged on her earlobe his hands were busy at her waistband, and all too soon she was wearing only her briefs and the narrow bra that was no cover at all. Her hands fluttered aimlessly over her breasts and he laughed softly as he removed them, placing them around his own lean waist. "I've seen you in less," he told her.

"That doesn't make this any more acceptable." Stern words, but their meaning was lost in the breathless whisper that escaped her lips.

"I find this"—he unhooked the lacy scrap and eased it from her arms—"even more acceptable." Then, with a deepening of his voice so that it registered on every nerve in her wanton body, he groaned, "Lacy, sweetheart, do you know what you're doing to me?"

The very feel of his breath on her naked breasts set fire to her, and when his mouth came down on one small pink nipple to caress it slowly with his tongue, she cried out, a small sound that relinquished every painfully learned lesson she had collected over the years. It all flew out the window in this storm of mindless sensation, and a force more relentless than any she had ever experienced took over. Unsteady hands slipped beneath her, lifting her, positioning her, and she could feel every beat of their combined hearts in the meeting of damp, warm flesh.

"Let me, darling . . . I won't hurt you," he breathed hoarsely.

Her only answer was to move her body even closer, and when she felt his hand go to his belt she knew there was no turning back. If she were to leave him tomorrow, never to see him again, at least she'd have this—this tremulous, raging ecstasy that promised sensations she could only imagine.

Had her own beginnings been prompted by such a terrible force? Was this why she had been born months too soon to a couple who were wildly unsuited? Was it a virus that got into the bloodstream, striking at random with disastrous results?

The thought crept into her mind and she felt some of the fire leave her. Her head turned to the wall and as if he sensed her withdrawal, Jordan paused and stared down at her from eyes that were almost black. "Darling? What is it?" His hand came up to her cheek and he turned her face up so that he could search for what had slipped unobtrusively between them. "Lacy? You do want this, don't you? Darling, I'm not an amateur . . . I don't make mistakes about something like this. Trust me."

She stared up at him with swimming eyes, all her emotions laid bare for him to read if he chose. "It isn't a matter of trust," she told him.

"And it isn't a time for words." He drew her up against him once more, but this time she resisted. With some vestige of sanity she held back, even when his hands began moving unerringly with a skill born of instinct and experience over her body. Instead of angering him, as she feared, her withdrawal only seemed to puzzle him. "Lacy? I won't take you against your will—you know that—but, sweetheart, your head and your body are telling different tales, and one of them doesn't lie."

This time the anger was on her part. She didn't know whether it was directed at him or at her own weakness, but when she sat up abruptly, he moved to allow her the freedom she demanded. He even handed her the blouse and helped her to put it on again, for her own hands were trembling to the point of ineffectiveness.

"All right, suppose you get it off your chest," he said with a heavy sigh of resignation. He seemed to have far more control over himself than she did; his hands were steady, his breathing only slightly ragged, and the steely glint in his eyes held something she had never seen there before, something that made her want to curl up and hide from what had to be said.

Her mouth felt dry. She opened it to speak and then cleared her throat and tried again, but it was no good. "I can't talk here, Jordan," she agonized.

"Do you want to go topside?" He was still half lying across the bunk, his shoulders against the bulkhead, and there was a fine film of perspiration gleaming on the silky skin of his torso above the low-riding velvety-soft jeans.

From her position at the head of the bunk, with her legs curled around at her side, Lacy tried to look away from him and failed. As if he were a magnet, her eyes were drawn to that chest that her hands had kneaded, those shoulders she had pulled down until they covered her own.

"Well? I must admit, I'm pretty darn curious as to what's so important!" He bit off the words coldly.

She looked directly into his face then, imploring him to try to understand, "It's my mother, Jordan."

"Your mother, for heaven's sake! What has—"

"If you're going to keep interrupting I can't tell you!"

"All right! All right! Lessons learned at mother's knee, number one—please continue."

She pushed at him then, tears of anger and frustration springing to her eyes. "Oh, go to the devil!"

"I'll meet you there," he flung back grimly, twisting away and standing. From a position uncomfortably high above her, he glared down, mockery radiating from eyes of blue flame. "I'm going over to the *Star*. I feel a strong need of some adult company for a change."

The door slammed after him and his feet sounded on the companionway, and by the time she thought to yell after him, "I'll just bet you do!" he had already cranked up the outboard on the dinghy. They usually just used the paddles, but this time he evidently needed the powerful roar as an outlet for his temper.

Well, she needed one, too! Glaring around the cabin, her eyes lit on the plastic hairbrush and she reached for it, feeling in advance the immense satisfaction she'd find in throwing it as hard as she could at the door. But before her fingers even closed over the fluorescent orange handle, she slumped, her hand falling limply at her side. No wonder Jordan had said he needed a little adult company for a change. It was bad enough to lead him on and then back out at the last minute—men were supposed to despise that sort of thing and she could well understand it—but to add a temper tantrum to that was inexcusable. Understandable, perhaps, but inexcusable.

The afternoon passed slowly, and Lacy fluctuated from periods of maudlin self-pity to energetic self-disgust. In between the extremes she wondered how she was expected to get ashore to check into the hotel. Jordan had said she wouldn't be staying at the hotel, but surely he didn't expect her to remain docilely on board until he came back from visiting his girl friend—*if* he came back.

She wondered wistfully if the others had gone to visit the ruin at the other end of the island. She would have liked to see at least one Mayan ruin before she went back home. After all, that had been the reason for the trip in the first place.

Several hours later Jordan paddled back to the sloop. Lacy was curled up on top of the cabin with a shriveled apple and a book that she had been unable to read more than a few words of—and those few over and over.

"Still here?" he asked shortly just before ducking into the hatch.

"Obviously," she muttered to herself, slamming the book shut and stretching out on her stomach as if she expected great things from the setting sun. No "What have you been doing with yourself, Lacy?" or "Wish you'd been with us today, Lacy." She might as well have hitched a ride ashore with one of the Mexican fishermen who kept their colorful boats along the stretch of beach nearby.

As an idea slowly formed in her mind, Lacy raised her head to stare out over the water. The *Phoenix* gently swung around on her two mooring lines so that she had a clear view of the shore, with its scattered boats, the row of palm trees, and, just across the boulevard that ran along the waterfront, the Posada Del Mar. She turned her head to study the catamaran that had anchored nearby only an hour ago.

Chapter Six

For good measure, she waited fifteen minutes after Jordan had disappeared aboard the *Star*. Her resolve was only hardened by the easy way he had accepted her decision not to join the others for dinner. He had seemed relieved, in fact, telling her to help herself to the contents of the galley.

After over a week of sailing, the cold storage was all but empty except for the milk and cheese and wine he had bought ashore. If she had had any doubts about picking up her reservation at the hotel and leaving Jordan, or even Lolene, to pay the tab, they dispersed as she glared angrily at the empty shelves.

The owner of the catamaran was a young Mexican archaeology student from Mérida who was having a last fling before returning to the University of Mexico at Mexico City. When she introduced herself and explained that her transportation ashore had been delayed indefinitely and that she had to check in before her reservations were surrendered, he flashed her a white smile and began untying the rubber raft he towed along behind.

"Pepe Vascos de Palanco can think of no more delightful way to spend an evening than escorting Miss Davis ashore. You must allow me to take you to dinner, Miss Davis," he told her gravely, subduing the sparkle in his mellow dark eyes. "My uncle owns the finest restaurant on the island and he would be heartbroken if I failed to bring you with me."

She laughed as he took her two parcels and helped her into the unstable raft. His outrageous courtliness was definitely not to be taken seriously and it suddenly seemed extremely important to her to spend an evening with someone with whom she could relax and enjoy herself. Pepe was an attractive young man. Not in the same league as Jordan, of course, but then she was through trying to hold her own against men of Jordan's caliber. From now on she'd stick to boys she could handle, and in spite of the open appreciation in Pepe's eyes, she had no doubts of her ability to come through the evening unscathed.

Her room had been reserved by a Miss MacArthur, and if the clerk thought it odd that she should be checking in with only two paper bags he refrained from mentioning it. She was given a room facing the water in one of the smaller units and Pepe promised to collect her within an hour.

"We must walk, you understand, but then that is part of the charm of the island—an evening stroll is a way of life in many Mexican towns, although not so much in your North American cities, I'm thinking."

She was used to walking, back home in Buics Creek, of course, but it was more a matter of economy than of entertainment.

On her one previous venture onto the island Lacy

97

had learned that jeans were almost de rigueur for tourists at any time of day and so she was able to dress in her own things with the exception of her blouse. Small enough satisfaction but at least she didn't have to feel under such an obligation to Jordan every minute of the evening. She intended to forget him for a few hours, at least.

Pepe was good company, interested in learning all about her and willing to answer her questions about the island. He was amused at her delight over the rose-red streets, used more for walking than for driving, and he told her an involved story about a slaver and pirate named Fermin Mundaca de Marechaja who met and fell madly in love with one Prisca Gomez and was determined to win her by building the largest, most prosperous plantation in all of Quintana Roo in the early 1860s. He never won the girl, but the remains of his ambitious estate were to be seen even now, if one knew just where to look.

The story carried them all the several blocks to the restaurant and then Pepe proceeded to interpret the menu for her, recommending so many dishes that in the end she surrendered and allowed him to choose for her. He overrode her laughing objection to barracuda and insisted on ordering several kinds of seafood for her to sample, along with a fish soup, a papaya frappé, and a Mexican wine she found delicious.

She met his uncle, his aunt, and several cousins, none of whom spoke English, and as the evening lengthened, she tried to subdue the small murmur of disquiet in the back of her mind. It wasn't as if Jordan could have any legitimate objection to her moving ashore. After all, since he had failed in his attempt to seduce her earlier, he had obviously washed his hands of her. If he needed more adult company, then she in turn needed to be with someone who didn't threaten the mores she had lived by all her life.

Purely in the interests of guiding her through the crowded streets, Pepe caught at her hand as they wandered across the square after dinner. She had sampled some of everything and between them they had demolished the bottle of wine, so when he suggested they sit awhile on a bench under a cluster of palms, she readily agreed. A crowd had gathered to watch a film in Spanish being shown on the facade of a building and in another direction the sounds of a noisy, cheerful circus could be heard and they began to see couples and family groups hurrying to the fairgrounds at the south end of the island, only a block or so from Lacy's hotel.

"Shall we?" Pepe inquired, his liquid brown eyes alight with devilment.

Lacy was still considering whether or not to extend the evening further—the wine and the dinner were resting uneasily on her stomach—when a voice from behind her sent a shiver of apprehension down her spine.

"If you're quite ready now, Lacy, I'll take you back to the *Phoenix*," Jordan intoned evenly.

She halted in her tracks and her head went back on her neck, her eyes closing with a feeling that was oddly like relief. It was as if she had been waiting all evening for the other shoe to drop.

Still she rebelled. "I'm registered at the hotel, Jordan. Thanks for the offer."

In the face of his waiting silence she had to introduce the two men, and she was uncomfortably aware of Jordan's arrogant scrutiny of the younger man.

"Pepe's aboard the catamaran moored next to the *Phoenix*," she offered with a cheerfulness that was purely contrived. "He offered me transportation ashore and was nice enough to take me out to his uncle's restaurant for dinner." She was chattering and couldn't seem to stop herself as a shiver of nerves caught up with her.

"How very kind of him," Jordan said mockingly. "If you're ready now, we'll get your things. I've planned an early day for us tomorrow and we'd better be turning in." Leaving Lacy gaping, he turned and nodded to the younger man. "Thanks for looking after her for me. Hope you enjoy your stay here."

By the time she was back aboard the *Phoenix*, Lacy was almost beyond words. Jordan had dealt with the hotel people and Pepe alike, with depressingly quiet efficiency. Within ten minutes she was back in the dinghy being carried out to the sloop that rocked gently at anchor in a sea of reflected lights. The fragrant breeze that rustled the palms was balmy, but Lacy was shivering by the time she climbed aboard the sailboat— shivering and perfectly furious at Jordan's high-handedness!

She turned to him before he had even finished securing the dinghy. "Well! Of all the rude, interfering—"

"That's enough," he interposed. He whipped the standing end of the painter around the cleat and swung his long khaki-clad legs aboard. "I suggest you get yourself to bed. By the looks of you, you've had more than enough to drink tonight—which makes two nights in a row, if I'm not mistaken." His voice was flatly unemotional.

The combined effects of the dinner, the wine, and Jordan's overbearing action drained Lacy's face of all color, leaving only the few freckles and her enormous gray-green eyes to relieve her pallor as she stood trembling beside the tiller.

With a cold, dark flame smoldering in his blue eyes Jordan moved closer to her, accusation in the very tilt of his head. "How were you planning to pay for your dinner—or need I ask?"

Blindly, she swung at him and her hand connected solidly with his hard cheek. He could have stopped her. She knew for a fact that his reflexes were lightning fast, but for some reason he allowed her to strike him, seemed almost to invite it.

Afterward, they stood facing each other only inches apart, the air between them shimmering with unvoiced tension. It built until she felt like screaming at him. She almost wished he would strike her back—anything except rake her unmercifully with those freezing eyes of his! His very control robbed her of her ability to fight further until she slumped, her shoulders drooping and her face crumpling and when a small sob escaped her he caught her shoulders with a rough sort of tenderness and turned her in the direction of her cabin. "All right. You gave it a try—now get to bed before I forget all my good intentions," he ordered gruffly.

She slept almost immediately, only to awaken several hours later in miserable confusion. For several long minutes she lay there in her bunk before she determined that she was *not* suffering the effects of a nightmare; her head really *was* pounding and her stomach queazy and she was drenched in clammy perspiration. A bug of some sort was definitely using her body as a battleground.

She stumbled into the head and located the aspirin, only to drop the bottle on the floor. By the time she had conquered the childproof lid and swallowed a dose, she was shaken by a chill. Back in her cabin, she fumbled in one of the paper bags and pulled out her sweater, tugging it on over her T-shirt, and then she climbed back into bed and drew herself up into a defensive ball, staring miserably at the teak paneling. She should have put on her jeans as well, but she lacked the strength or the resolution to get out of bed again. Tremors racked her body as she waited for the medicine to take effect. Was it the wine, as Jordan had hinted, or perhaps the food? Was this the way that bane of travelers, *turista*, was supposed to strike?

She supposed it could be worse—but not very much. Even in the darkness she was aware of visual disturbances.

"Lacy? What's going on?" Jordan called softly through the door.

Oh, darn! As if she weren't suffering enough! "Go away," she groaned.

He entered, leaving the door open behind him so that the streetlights from shore shown through from the cabin across from hers. "Honey, what is it?"

He sounded genuinely concerned, she thought rancorously, which only proved how deceptive he could be—or how gullible *she* could be. "It's only a headache," she grumbled weakly as a fresh surge of tremors raked through her.

His hand was on her forehead. "Headaches alone don't usually bring on chills and fever. What else hurts?"

"Nothing! What did you expect—my conscience?"

In the dim light she could see his strong teeth gleaming whitely. "Well, it's a cinch your temper isn't immune. How's the tummy?"

"The tummy's just perfect," she told him grudgingly. "All I need is a blanket and to be left alone."

The blanket was already drifting down over her and he waited, his hand on her forehead, while she glared balefully into the gloomy light. She refused to look at him, refused to even thank him. In her stricken condition she managed to blame him for all her troubles. Her knees were drawn up practically to her chin and still she was cold, with a chill that started somewhere deep inside her and worked its way out.

With a muffled exclamation, Jordan scooped her up, blanket and all, and swung her around to the door. She caught at the doorframe. "Where are you taking me?" she cried wildly.

"Somewhere where I can get you warm again. Shut up and close your eyes," he growled, striding swiftly into his own room with her. He managed to place her on his bed despite her uncoordinated attack on him, but when he followed her under the covers, dragging her up against his warm body, she wailed, "Darn you, Jordan Stone, why can't you just leave me alone? I *hate* you! I hope I can forget I ever *met* you once this nightmare trip is done with!"

He was totally still for an instant. It was almost as if she could feel the shock of her words striking at that large, rock-hard body, but then he turned her on her side, easing her spine up to his front as he cupped her in his arms. "Once I let you go, we'll both do our best to forget."

Amazingly enough, sleep came upon her within minutes. With the heat of his body to uncoil her rigid muscles, she was able to relax and allow the aspirin to do its work. If her dreams were troubled, they soon faded away as she slowly regained consciousness the next morning.

Something had roused her. For several moments she lay still and listened, but all she heard was Jordan's slow, regular breathing from beside her. They had separated in the night, but one of his arms was flung across her waist and she became slowly aware that one of his legs was tangled with hers.

Moving carefully so as not to disturb him, she tried to

ease herself away, lifting his wrist and placing his arm beside her on the bed. It was amazing how heavy an arm could be. His leg was another matter, though, it was holding down her bottom leg and without a major upheaval there was little she could do. Already he was beginning to sigh in his sleep.

Something bumped against the hull, rocking it gently, and the noise finished the job. He stretched slowly and then murmured her name as he pulled her back up against his body. "Hmmmm, I thought I must be dreaming, but that's real enough." One hand had moved unerringly to her breast and he closed his fingers slowly on the sensitive flesh.

"Let me up, Jordan."

"Don't be foolish," he mocked sleepily. "Why should I do that?"

Her nerve endings were supersensitive, as if they could taste and touch and smell and feel, and with the awareness that her headache was now gone came an awareness of another sort altogether. "Jordan, let me go." She meant, Let me get away from you, away from this bed in this sloop, away from this island to where I can start to seal off all the disturbing memories.

"Doesn't that sweater itch? Let me help you . . ."

She pulled away and he caught her and jerked her back into his arms.

"Jordan!" she cried, vexed and frightened of her own traitorous reaction to his nearness. It was gradually becoming very evident to her that he had on very little in the way of clothing. If he had been angry with her last night—and there could be little doubt of that—then there was no sign of his anger now. Instead a playful sort of mood was upon him and it occurred to her that he was far more dangerous now than he had been the night before when he had allowed her to get away with striking him.

"I told you I had an early start in mind, didn't I?" he murmured against her ear. "Are you feeling up to a full day's activity? No headache?" His fingers were playing games on the bare skin between her sweater and her lacy nylon bikini pants and she wriggled away to the extent that he'd let her—which wasn't very far.

"Why won't you . . ." she began when the sound of someone boarding the sloop came clearly through the paneling.

"Jordan! Darling, where are you?" Lolene called gaily. The sound of her high heels rang out clearly on the polished deck. "Did you know your little playmate has flown the coop? I called over at the—"

The scene would have been funny under other circumstances. Lacy could almost bring herself to smile at the look of utter stupefaction on the beautiful face as the blonde threw open the door to Jordan's cabin and caught sight of them in the bed together.

Give her credit for a rapid recovery. The mouth closed firmly, the glint in those pale eyes hidden by a sweep of thick black lashes, and she even managed a small laugh. "Are we being treated to a bedroom farce or is this a trade-off for old I.O.U.s?"

Lacy felt like pulling the spread up over her head, but Jordan didn't even bother to remove the arm that was holding her against him.

"If you'd care to wait outside, Lolene, we'll join you in a few minutes," he said quietly. Either this was extreme courage under fire or he was no stranger to such scenes.

Torn between absurd urges either to laugh and cry, Lacy thrust her chin forward and gritted her teeth. It would pass. Soon she'd be able to put it all behind her and try to pretend none of it had ever happened.

Lolene went without another word and Lacy struggled to sit up, only to be pulled back down unceremoniously. When she turned her head to express her outrage, Jordan caught her off guard and kissed her—a brief, hard kiss that drained away the little courage she had found.

"Did you have to do that?" she demanded unreasonably. "Why didn't you just leave me alone in the first place and then none of this mess would ever have happened?"

"If I'd left you alone in the first place, where do you think you'd be by now?" he asked reasonably. "Or maybe you mean in the second place—or even the third?" He quirked an eyebrow at her just as if he hadn't compromised them both with his fiancée.

"This is ridiculous! I'm going to get up and get dressed and then I'm going to Cancún and get my papers and take the first thing out of here that flies!"

"Purely as a matter of interest, how do you propose to do all that?"

She frowned, pausing momentarily with one foot on the deck and one still under the covers, brushing cozily up against the hairy leg that had captured it. "It won't be much of a problem, believe me," she retorted grimly, thinking that if Lolene had been anxious to see the last of her yesterday, how much more so she'd be at this moment!

While Jordan slipped into his clothes and went on deck, Lacy assumed to try to placate his fiancée, she closed the door of her own cabin behind her, and for several long moments all she could do was clasp her face with both hands while she stared at the brilliant sunlight coming through the porthole. Last night's misery was nothing compared to what she felt this morning. She heartily wished she had never set eyes on Jordan or the Island of Women or Lolene—most of all, Lolene MacArthur. How on earth was she going to face the woman's sly, condemning look and find the nerve to ask for her help?

But it wasn't Lolene who greeted her when she finally steeled herself to go outside. There was no sign of either Jordan or the tall Texas beauty; instead Tad and Jenny bade her a good morning with no more than a slightly lifted eyebrow. Jenny proceeded to tell her that yesterday's plans to visit the ruins had been postponed until today so as to have time enough to take in the sights along the way.

"If you're game, you can ride a wild turtle," Tad offered. "Or at least bet on which of us can stay on long enough to reach the other end of the compound. Hey! That's it! We'll have a real Texas-style rodeo!"

It was decided, and somehow Lacy found herself one of the crowd of a dozen who took the three launches belonging to the *Star* and headed north along the coast. Grabbing up her bathing suit and a towel, she decided fatalistically that she might as well go along, since it looked as if her chances of getting to Cancún would have to wait.

Through no obvious manipulation that she could observe, Lolene accompanied Jordan, Tad, and Jenny in one boat while Lacy boarded the next one along with Naylor and a couple who bickered constantly. They were followed by still a third. Each was manned by a uniformed crew member who saw to loading aboard the ice chests of drinks and snacks as well as a supply of snorkeling equipment.

The drone of the inboard was hypnotizing as they skimmed across the water to swerve around the low arm of land that protected the bay. Conversation was difficult and after the first few attempts Naylor fell silent and Lacy was left to stare out over the incredible

colors of the water—the turquoise shading into ultramarine and back again—to the faint smudge on the
horizon that was the mainland. Her thoughts were
confused as she tried to determine at just what point
she had lost control of her life.

Had it been when she fell in love with Jordan?
No—that had not been a sudden thing but a slow,
imperceptible warming that had boiled over before she
recognized it for what it was. When she first set foot on
the *Phoenix* then?

Might as well go on back to the moment she had
landed in Belize City, or before that even—when Aunt
Lottie had presented her with the trip as a fait accompli
—ticket, companion, itinerary, and all.

The launch ahead of them picked up speed once it
gained the open water and she stared at the tall form
standing beside the helmsman. Lolene had tried to
stand beside him and had given up after nearly falling,
but neither wind nor water had the slightest effect on
Jordan's rugged strength as he shifted his weight subtly
to maintain his balance. The faded blue denim shirt
billowed out from his broad shoulders, giving him a
hunched look, and the sharp wind produced by the
speed whipped his pants around those cleanly muscled
thighs and calves, accenting the narrow hips in a way
that Lacy found impossible to ignore. One hand was
resting lightly on the console, the other hooked into his
belt, and he seemed to be chatting with the crewman
despite the roar of the engine.

The sudden cut of speed took her unawares. She had
been studying Jordan instead of the coastline and now
she saw they had arrived at a wooden pier that jutted
out from the creamy sand of the palm-shaded beach.
Open native huts dotted the area and there were
several rows of chairs, rusted through in most cases,

behind which fluttered clotheslines of colorful garments resembling enormous butterflies, supposedly for sale.

Naylor assisted her in climbing out onto the pier and she hastily averted her eyes from a pair of topless sun bathers, one of which was female, who were using the pier as their private playground.

The turtle pens were on either side of the pier, and as the others congregated and began jostling each other as they pointed out various of the impounded seagoing reptiles, placing bets and making dares, Lacy found herself backed up against the hard, reassuring form of Jordan.

"Going to give it a try, Lacy?"

She shook her head slowly, uttering a small, broken laugh as she declined. "I'd as soon hook a ride on a roller coaster—blindfolded."

"No sense of adventure, hmmm?" he teased.

"No death wish," she corrected, wishing she were more in control of her breathing apparatus. She was afraid he'd notice the small shallow gasps and she tried to move away.

He leaned over to speak against her ear. "Don't make the mistake of playing around with Morningstar. He's lethal where sweet young things are concerned."

Using her irritation as an excuse, she planted an elbow against his solar plexus and shoved. "Give me credit for some good sense, at least!"

His hand slid down from her shoulder to her elbow and he crushed the tender flesh against her bones as he growled softly, "When I've seen evidence of it, maybe I will. Until then you'll be guided by what I say."

His grim words were interrupted by Lolene's husky drawl. "Honey love, we're riding in the first heat. Go put on your spurs while I fetch us a daiquiri for courage."

With no more than a swift warning glance at Lacy Jordan moved off, and to Lacy's dismay the blond Texan lingered to issue a warning of her own. "You've had your fling, so suppose we arrange for you to go to Cancún as soon as we get back to the *Star*. Surely your papers will be waiting at the airport and the immigration officials there can fix you up with a tourist card to get you back home. If you've already spent everything Jordan gave you, then I'll spring for a one-way ticket."

Lacy overcame a sudden impulse to shove the cool, elegant woman off the pier. "Thanks, but Jordan will look after things for me."

Pale blue eyes grew strangely opaque. "I didn't think you were overburdened with pride, but believe me, honey, even someone like you should be smart enough to get out before you become a complete laughing-stock. Oh, I'm not saying Jordan won't be willing to take whatever you're willing to give—at least until he grows bored—but take it from someone who's known him a long time, his attention span is definitely limit-ed!" Her pink frosted mouth was open to continue when Tad and Jenny moved away from the noisy crowd and tugged at her arm and Lacy was spared further humiliation.

The reptile rodeo was a comedy of errors. If the decibel level was anything to go by, then it was an overwhelming success. Lacy, content to swing her legs from the pier and watch the unpredictable antics, decided that at least half of the purpose seemed to be the inadvertent baring of bodies when someone grabbed a handhold that turned out to be a shoulder strap or a bra tie. Tad was a hands-down champ in that department.

It wasn't until the pen was filled with churning bodies trying to grab a tail or a flipper or the edge of a carapace and then hang on for a brief ride before the turtle submerged that Lacy realized Jordan was not a part of the merriment. Nor was Lolene, for all her challenge. The pair of them were on shore in the shade of a thatched shelter, with frosty daiquiris in hand and Lacy, sweltering in the midday sun, jutted her chin belligerently, wishing she had sought the shade before they did, for there was no way she could saunter up and join them.

From there they went on to Garrafon, the next beach establishment, for snorkeling along the inshore reefs. There was an attractive open-sided restaurant and someone prevailed upon the management to supply an enormous pile of cracked lobster on crushed ice, which they ate in the hot sunshine with the juice dripping from arms and fingers, washing the delectable feast down with cold *cerveza* or white wine.

Lacy was self-conscious as she sat on the edge of the group and nibbled the succulent shellfish. She had chosen a soft drink, not daring to take on more alcohol after last night, even if she had wanted to. The others seemed to have no such inhibitions, and by the time the pile was reduced to a mound of empty shells, the others, with a few notable exceptions, seemed to veer between drowsiness and noisy high spirits.

One exception was Naylor, who remained apart from the others, watching all activities without actually taking part in any of them. It was as if he were merely interested in studying the characteristics of an experimental group under various conditions, entering in only when it became necessary to encourage them.

Jordan's words came back to her—Naylor Morningstar could be lethal. She subdued a shudder and pulled her shirt more closely around her pink shoulders. In

111

spite of her hard-earned tan, too large a dose at once left decidedly pinkish overtones that were uncomfortable later.

The other exception was Jordan. He had held a glass in one hand during a large part of the past hour or so, but it had gradually occurred to Lacy that she had yet to see him take a drink. She had watched him surreptitiously and had been surprised to see his eyes on her far more than chance would explain.

He was watching *her* as well! Over the heads of the others, while Lolene was talking softly to him, while he was picking out morsels of lobster—whenever his eyes moved across the group in a seemingly careless swing, they settled on her for a long, burning instant and it felt to Lacy as if she were scarred by their fleeting touch.

Restlessly she lowered her glass and turned to Jenny. "Are we going to get to see the ruin, do you think?"

The small redhead, swaddled in an oversized cotton sweatshirt, licked off her fingers as she shrugged. "If it calls for any exertion, I'd say not. Lo's calling the shots and she wouldn't walk across the street for a fire sale at Tiffany's."

Tad leaned across. "We might run on out to the point in boats. You can get a view of the thing, at least. Nothing to see but a pile of rocks anyway."

The comment was picked up by one of the others and it was soon agreed that they would pile into the three boats for a cruise around the southern end of the island to glimpse the small Mayan ruin. From there on, it was decided, those who had the energy and desire could climb a ladderlike stairway on the bay side and walk the few hundred remaining yards for a closer look.

This time Lacy was in the boat with Jordan. She didn't quite know how it had come about, but she was quite certain it was a surprise to the blond Texan, and not a welcome one at that, judging from the malevolent glare she threw Lacy's way as they pulled away from the pier.

The trip took only minutes through the crystal-clear water and Lacy was entranced to see the same colorful fish she had seen the day she had snorkeled with Jordan, only slightly dimmed by the surface refraction, swimming idly about the mooring place when they neared the sheer, rocky cliff.

Several of the more daring members of the party decided to make the climb, Lacy among them, and she carefully avoided looking to see if Jordan were following the single-file ascent or remaining behind to placate his girl friend.

Once over the top of the ladder, she forgot both Jordan and Lolene in her breathless delight at the scene before her. Not even the camera-burdened Japanese couple or the bearded biker who was leaning back astride his rented bike dousing his shoulders with suntan oil could dim her excitement in the view.

The ruin was incredibly small, even for such a tiny island. A temple, according to Jordan, it had withstood the centuries clinging precariously to the very edge of a precipice. The sea—so calm and beguiling on the protected bay side—dashed furious waves at the base, like hungry green and white monsters reaching desperately for sustenance.

She turned to speak to the nearest person and discovered that, while some had gone ahead, some already had begun the descent. She trotted over the rugged trail, sidestepping swathes of cactus and sandspurs. Small rocks rolled under her feet and she thanked providence she had worn her sneakers instead of the more flattering macrame sandals. Just as she reached the ruined temple, Jordan called after her.

"Lacy! Didn't you wear a hat?"

Startled, she whirled around, almost coming to grief

on the uneven surface. "Jordan, I didn't know you were coming. A hat?"

"Your nose is watermelon pink," he said, grinning, catching up with her as his long-legged stride swung easily from rock to rock. He threw an arm across her shoulder and they passed one of the couples in their party who had evidently had enough. The man called after them. "Hey, Stone, we're going to get up a load and head on back to the *Star*."

Jordan nodded briefly and then urged Lacy up to the very base of the stone building. "Pity nothing's been done to preserve it, but then there are dozens on Cozumel in as bad shape, if not worse. I'll give you a hand up if you want to go inside. The east wall's gone—looks as if the whole cliff fell into the sea." He took her hand and Lacy climbed up the huge rectangular blocks of stone, leaning over as she ducked inside the small enclosure. Jordan was right behind her and there was no room to do more than turn around. He brushed against her and then, when she leaned forward to peer out over the partially tumbled south wall, he caught her back against him.

"I can't get over it," she breathed, half choked with a strange emotion that was a combination of the surroundings and the nearness of the man who held her unnecessarily close. She could actually feel the easy beat of his heart against her shoulder and his breath stirred the tendrils of hair at her temple. "Look how tiny the boats look," she whispered.

"You don't have to lower your voice," he told her, a smile in his own, "but I understand what you're feeling. There's a presence here."

Looking down on the brilliant seascape below, it was all too easy to imagine it in a storm, with a blackened sky driving mountainous breakers against the fallen base and bolts of jagged lightning threatening the vulnerable temple. She shuddered and instantly Jordan's hands tightened on her shoulders.

"You're too sensitive to the ambience," he murmured, his mouth against her ear.

Lacy honestly couldn't have said if her reaction had to do with the charged atmosphere inside the cramped space or with Jordan's touch, his breath warming the side of her face in the rather dank stone building. His hands moved slowly over her shoulders and his fingers brushed the swell of her breasts and then they were startled by the sound of nearby laughter as another group from the launches approached the temple ruins.

"Hi, how about vacating and making room for somebody else," Tad sang out from below them.

There was an immediate shuffling and as soon as Jordan lowered Lacy to the ground Lolene demanded to be taken inside. With several others waiting to explore the ruin, Lacy wandered away, pausing to study the more modern monument nearby with its Spanish inscription. As the party wandered back and forth across the peninsula, she edged closer to the seaward side, fascinated by the rugged terrain as well as the frigate birds that soared over the rocks. Further out she spotted a school of bottle-nosed dolphin, and then, seeing something that looked as if it might be another ruin, she made her laborious way over the rocks, skirting the rugged growth that clung to the thin soil.

The remains of the estate poor Fermin de Marechaja built for his lady love, Prisca, was supposed to be somewhere on this end of the island, according to Pepe. Wouldn't it be marvelous if she discovered it all by herself?

After narrowly escaping a serious fall and sliding twice, scraping her knees and hands, Lacy discovered that her "ruin" was only another outcropping of the indigenous gray rock. Disappointed, she carefully turned around on the narrow shelf of level ground that clung to the side of a sheer drop and edged her way back, extremely aware of the heat, the dust, and the way her skin was beginning to protest both the sunburn and the scratches. She'd be a real mess by the time she got back to the launches. It would be just her luck for these weeds to turn out to be the Mexican equivalent of poison ivy!

Reaching the plateau again, she veered toward the ruin but, seeing no one in that vicinity, turned to study the nearby lighthouse building. It seemed deserted, as well, except for a few chickens, so she began the trek across to the ladder. She only hoped they weren't impatient with her for holding them up while she went off on a wild-goose chase.

One launch had already returned to the *Star*—perhaps another one as well by now. She began to jog. By the time she reached the ladder she was quite out of breath and she paused only an instant to call out to the boat below that she was on her way.

Only there wasn't a boat below.

Climbing halfway down the ladder, she swung around to stare in both directions. Nothing! Halfway across the bay to Cancún a large sailboat broke the reddening sky, but that was all.

They must have cruised around the point looking for her on the other side—that was it! But should she go back and try to hail them or wait here on the narrow beach? It would be just her luck to miss them if she climbed up again and ran across the top.

She swallowed a small niggle of uncertainty. Not panic—there was certainly nothing to panic over. Lolene might delight in a chance to leave her marooned on the uninhabited end of the island, but certainly with three boatloads she wouldn't dare. And if she did, she wouldn't get away with it.

Oh, Lacy, don't be paranoid! Nobody's planning your demise from exposure on a deserted tropical island. Besides, one doesn't get lost on an island that's only five miles long. One gets blisters from walking home, perhaps, but not lost. Not *lost* lost.

Chapter Seven

It was little more than a kilometer, at best, to where the hard surfaced road began, but to Lacy, hurrying over the rocky, irregular trail that sloped off on each side to an impenetrable low growth, it seemed endless. She had no way of knowing how far she would have to go over that terrain and it was fast growing dark. She had waited at the ruin for perhaps half an hour or more in case someone returned to look for her, but when sullen purple clouds began to block out the last coppery rays of the sunset she decided it was foolish to wait longer.

She passed no one. The gracklelike birds she had seen squabbling in the palm trees were the only sign of life she encountered—unless one counted the ambiguous rustlings from the undergrowth that prompted her footsteps to hurry even more.

Wild flowers dotted the foliage. An hour before she had inhaled their fragrance appreciatively. Now, with darkness robbing them of color, they were like pale eyes, gleaming at her mockingly. By the time she crested the final hill and came upon the hard pavement, her breath was coming in sobbing gasps.

There was a shelter of sorts, a taxi stand, probably, serving the Garrafon beach area, only it was deserted now. No lights gleamed from the restaurant and no taxis were awaiting their fares. Not even a bicycle was propped against the peeled logs that supported the thatched roof.

Even in the dim light of the handful of stars that remained visible the pavement was discernible and so she started out boldly, whistling tunelessly to keep up her flagging spirits. Perhaps the bus she had seen trundling back and forth along the waterfront boulevard would soon be along. She hadn't the fare, for her money was aboard the launch, but that wouldn't prevent her from getting on. Once seated, she defied any soft-spoken, ultrapolite Mexican bus driver to eject her.

As she panted up the steep hills, brushing away the hoards of hungry mosquitos, her emotions veered from the extremes of self-pity to anger, with several less easily definable stages in between. It was clear to see what had happened—each boatload thought she had returned with the other. Only why, once all three had returned and it became obvious that she was not among the party, hadn't *someone* returned for her? It would only have taken a matter of minutes.

Her head was so filled with half-formed speculations that she wasn't aware of the approaching vehicle until the sweep of headlights crested the hill and then she darted off to one side, shuddering as she stepped into a bush. Her raw imagination created snakes, lizards, and poisonous insects even before she considered the possibilities of being picked up alone, far from town on a dark night, by a stranger.

The vehicle—it was a truck—roared past, screeched to a halt, and began backing up to where she stood frozen in terror. Her mind wanted to run but her limbs held her immobilized. All the nightmare memories of her first day on foreign soil came back to overwhelm her, and by the time the door was flung open and the driver's dark form swung out within a few feet of her, she was frantically searching her mind for any self-defense techniques she could recall.

"Lacy, what the devil do you think you're doing?"

Her breath was expelled in a single, wondering word. "Jordan?"

She was scooped up and practically hurled into the truck before Jordan slammed the door after him and took off. Neither of them spoke until he had returned to the wide paved area by Garrafon beach, where he turned the truck around and headed back toward town at a suicidal rate of speed.

A plastic figurine gyrated on a magnetic base on the dashboard and she stared at it as if it were a talisman against the anger she could feel coming at her in waves from the silent figure beside her. Not until they swerved onto the municipal dock and came to a halt did she dare open her mouth.

"How did you—when did you . . ." she ventured timidly.

"Not now!" he barked at her, urging her along by one arm to where the dinghy was tied up. His voice was rough-edged with anger, but she had the oddest impression that anger was not the foremost thing on Jordan's mind just now. There was something she couldn't identify, and in her distressed condition she began to toy with the idea that Jordan had been more worried than she would have supposed.

They headed for the *Star* and her heart sank. The last thing she wanted now was to have to face the malicious amusement of that particular group. "Couldn't we just . . . ?"

"Wait here," he growled, tossing a half hitch around a bollard on the low floating dock at the *Star's* beam.

She waited, huddled on the cushioned thwart. The absence of sun, combined with her overexposure to its burning rays earlier, produced an uncomfortable coolness and she shivered as she scratched mosquito bites on her bare arms and legs. Irrelevantly, she remembered the image she had carried with her aboard the plane back home. A tanned, sexy version of Lacy Davis wandered dreamily along an exotic shore, her arms entwined with those of a tall, equally tanned hero type in white rolled-up jeans and a casual knit shirt. He would be beaming down at her in faceless adoration. She rather thought there had been the gleam of a gold medallion around his neck, nestling in the masculine thatch of hair on his chest.

Only now, instead of faceless adoration, the face was quite clear in her mind and the emotion was anything *but* adoration!

Jordan swung back aboard and yanked the painter free. Within minutes they were approaching the *Phoenix* and Lacy breathed a sigh of relief. Even Jordan's serrated tongue was more welcome than the cold blast of malice from Lolene's pale blue eyes. She had been treated to that more than once during the course of the day, starting with the rude awakening in Jordan's bed!

"Go inside and get a shower and put something on that sunburn. I'll see about something to eat," he ordered evenly. If she had thought she heard concern earlier under the anger, she must have been out of her mind. There was no sign of anything now other than disgust.

The thought of a cold shower wasn't altogether welcome, but she was sticky with salt and perspiration and probably caked with dust as well—not to mention liberally decorated with assorted scrapes, scratches, and bites. A figure more ludicrously different from the one of her earlier daydream would be hard to conjure up!

It was a quarter of an hour later, when she was sitting on the side of her bunk wrapped in a towel, that she noticed the unusual motion. With her mind poised between simply falling into bed or going into the galley for something to eat—it had been a long time since the lobsters she had had at Garrafon—it didn't register, at first, but when it did, she jumped to her feet. Clutching the towel around her, she darted into the area that was lounge, chart room, galley, and dining room combined and stuck her head out the hatch.

"What's going on here?" she demanded of Jordan, who was applying himself to the tiller as the sails cracked overhead.

"Get something on if you're coming out here."

She started to fling a reply at him, thought better of it, and subsided to throw on one of the loose cotton outfits of his she had worn before her own wardrobe had been enlarged.

"Now, would you be so good as to tell me just where you think you're going?" she blurted, coming back out to the dark cockpit a few minutes later. Her hair was dripping down her back, rapidly saturating the soft cotton shirt, and she shivered in the wind that stiffened the jib and bellied out the main.

Even in the darkness she was aware of his gleaming grin. "I thought I was doing you a favor by taking off tonight instead of waiting for you to demand your release."

That took some considering. Lacy paused while she

digested his reply and then ventured a foray in another direction. "Why did you all go off and leave me?"

Jordan adjusted the course instinctively to make the most of the wind. "It was accidental, I assure you—at least as far as I'm concerned. To tell the truth, I don't think Lo has your best interests at heart, so maybe she was a bit hasty in assuring me you'd gone back with an earlier boatload, but that's not important now that you're safely on your way, is it?" He was sprawled out, one arm lying along the tiller and both legs stretched out before him, and Lacy's suspicions grew as she tried to interpret his attitude of quiet satisfaction.

"On my way where?" she parried.

"First stop, Cancún. We'll get you all legalized first and go on from there."

"Tonight?" she marveled, not at all certain she appreciated the efficient way he was disposing of her problems.

"I doubt we'd be able to do much business tonight. I thought we might anchor off Puerta Juárez and head for the airport first thing in the morning."

Confused by the whole recent set of occurences, Lacy took refuge in something more concrete. "I'm awfully hungry. Have you had any dinner?"

Later, over thick steak sandwiches and mugs of coffee, Lacy tried to discover what had prompted Jordan's sudden decision to leave Isla Mujeres so abruptly. "If you'd waited a little longer," she told him, "you wouldn't have had to make the trip at all. Lolene offered to have the helicopter bring me across the bay. She even promised to lend me enough to buy a ticket home."

Jordan lifted one eyebrow sardonically. "Hmmm. Lo's pretty efficient when the spirit moves her." He didn't elaborate and Lacy gave her attention to her supper. There was little she could say that wouldn't reveal her opinion of his fiancée, and now that she was so near escape, there was nothing to be gained in playing the poor loser. She wasn't a loser, anyway—how could one lose what one had never had?

"Did you put something on your bites and burns?" Jordan asked mildly, pulling out one of his cheroots and settling in greater comfort on the cushioned locker.

She nodded, finding it suddenly difficult to speak. A lump was growing rapidly in her throat and it occurred to her that unless she made her escape immediately she was going to make an even greater fool of herself. "I . . . I think I'll go to bed. If . . . if you don't mind." Her voice sounded husky, but reasonably steady, especially in view of the fact that the light was haloing alarmingly as her eyes filled.

Turning swiftly, she placed her dishes on the counter to wash in the morning and edged out of the room. She halfway expected Jordan to call her back, at least to say goodnight, but he didn't. Not even when she heard him making his way to his own cabin, much later, did he so much as call out a quiet good night.

She was awake both late and early and the brief intervening hours of sleep were troubled. After plowing through hours of rationalizations, she finally concluded that Jordan's only desire was to get her off his hands before she made irreparable trouble between him and his intended. She had caused trouble all along the way.

No wonder he was unwilling to entrust her to anyone else when it came to seeing her onto a plane bound for the States! He probably thought that if he sent her across with the helicopter pilot, she'd somehow manage to miss her plane and beat the helicopter back to Isla Mujeres, landing herself on his doorstep once more.

The fragrant aroma of freshly made coffee penetrated her cabin and she stretched, experiencing only the slightest soreness from her adventures of the previous day. Her lips curled wryly as she once more dug out the familiar jeans and sweater—her traditional going-away outfit. With a certain amount of dismay she surveyed the enormous pile of coins and notes on the dresser. There were peso notes and coins in a bewildering number of denominations and she hadn't the slightest idea how much it amounted to in U.S. currency. She'd just have to trust to luck—and Jordan —to see that she had enough to get her home.

"Jordan," she greeted without preamble on emerging from her cabin, "you'll have to give me a forwarding address so I can send you the money you lent me. The bank at home will help me with my traveler's checks and—" Noticing his slanted look, she added hurriedly, "Oh, I know you only wanted to save me embarrassment by letting me think you'd redeemed them for me, but after all, even I know it's not that simple."

"Do you?" he mocked gently. "Come sit down and have some breakfast. The sooner we finish and get under way, the sooner you'll be duly registered among the ranks of law-abiding citizens."

She grimaced and, at the pain of her sunburned nose, grimaced even more.

Jordan laughed and poured her coffee. "Somehow I don't think it'll ever be the same cruising alone in any waters—especially these," he mused.

She shot him a swift look, unable to cover the surge of wistful hope that flared up and as quickly subsided. He wouldn't be cruising alone much longer. He'd have

Lolene for company, although try as she would, she couldn't imagine the elegant blonde being satisfied with a thirty-five-foot sloop when she could have something much more luxurious.

Irrationally irritated by the cheerful efficiency with which Jordan went about getting under way, Lacy slammed the dishes into the stainless steel sink and only their thick strength saved them. You'd think he'd have the grace not to be in such an all-fired hurry, now that he was going to be rid of her once and for all. A few more minutes wouldn't make that much difference.

"Don't you ever intend to go home and get to work like ordinary mortals?" she demanded a few minutes later when she joined him on deck. It was none of her business, besides which it was a thoroughly ill-bred question, but she suddenly hated everything about the man who was striving to dispatch her so heartlessly from his life. "I think it's a shame that a grown man like you can waste his lifetime puttering around in sailboats when the country's in such terrible economic shape!"

He blinked at her owlishly and then burst into laughter. The sharply angled sun beat down on his shaking shoulders as he set the vane steering mechanism and ambled across the few feet separating them. Without a word, he hauled her into his arms and smothered her outraged protests with a kiss that started as one thing and ended up as quite another.

Several minutes later it was a thoroughly shaken Lacy who heard Jordan say, "Lacy—what would you say if I asked you to stay with me?"

Warily, she eased away from his arms and he didn't try to hold her. There was something totally unreal about the scene, and with an unusual degree of objectivity Lacy considered it. A slightly rakish sloop moved silently on a course in waters of unbelievable color and clarity, under a sky that domed over them like a rainbow-hued bowl. A man in worn jeans and a white knit shirt stood, legs braced widely, staring expectantly down at her. A man unlike any she had ever met before, a man from a totally different world.

A man she had had the misfortune to fall in love with.

"Why?" she asked baldly.

He shrugged. "Why not?"

Shot through with a wild temptation to say yes, to close her eyes to the consequences, Lacy said, "That's no answer!"

This time it was Jordan who surveyed her warily. He moved to lean back against the rail, fingering a cleated sheet and unconsciously taking up slack with a calloused forefinger as his eyes ranged over her. "What sort of an answer would you believe? Do you want a commitment in writing?"

"Any commitment from you wouldn't be worth the paper it was written on," she retorted, stung to an unreasonable bitterness. Almost immediately she shook her head in denial. "No, that's not true. I'm sorry, Jordan. You've done more than anyone could expect for me and I want you to know I appreciate it. It's just that—oh, I don't know! Maybe I'm just homesick!" She laughed and the sound was more like a sob. "That's it—I've been away too long."

"You don't believe that for a single minute, and neither do I," Jordan said softly. He let the jib sheet go and the line twanged. "Lacy . . . what sort of ties do you have back home? Is there some fellow waiting for you to get your final fling over and done with before you settle down for keeps?"

Biting her bottom lip, Lacy eyed him thoughtfully. Was this some new game he had invented to keep her off balance till the last? "Why do you want to know?"

"No contract with a school ready to be taken up when you get back?"

Cautiously she admitted that the most she could hope for at the moment was substitute teaching, although she had more or less been promised an opening in February when one of the teachers left to have her baby.

"And the boyfriend?" he prompted. His eyes had never looked bluer or more guileless.

"There's no one really special," she admitted reluctantly. It would have done her ego good to be able to claim an impatient fiancé, but at this late date she doubted that he would have believed her.

"In that case," he said very gently, his eyes revealing nothing of his true feelings, "I can't think of a single reason why we don't call your aunt and tell her you'll be staying on indefinitely."

Her head flew back and she stared at him doubtfully. "Jordan, before you say anything else I think I'd better tell you that I'm not open to games of that sort. I know what you must think of me—I mean, I let you—well, once or twice I . . ." She could feel the slow color rising up to shame her and she forced herself to hold his enigmatic gaze while she found the right words to tell him she wasn't going to be another in his lineup of girl friends. "I don't know what happened between you and Lolene, but whatever it was, I don't intend to fill in until she gets around to marrying you. Nor will I hang around to salvage your ego if she turned you down," she concluded with far more firmness than she felt. Her legs felt as if they'd been suddenly rendered boneless and she backed up until the bench was behind her.

"Oh, and what makes you think she might have done that?" he inquired silkily.

"It's pretty darned evident," she blurted. "I mean, I'm here and she's not!"

"Irrelevant," he dismissed. "Maybe I decided not to ask her."

"And maybe you asked and she said not until you get rid of your excess baggage! Well, let me tell you something, Jordan Stone, you're no more anxious to get rid of me than I am to be got rid of! I've about had it with your—your lecherous propositions!"

A muscle twitched at the corner of his mouth. Other than that, Jordan revealed not a touch of emotion. "Lecherous? I rather had the idea we were something more like friends," he suggested mildly.

She dropped down onto the bench behind her and stared distrustfully across at him. Behind his head the sky was beginning to go pewter gray in spite of the brilliant slant of morning sunlight. "If your idea of a friend is someone you try to get into bed every chance you get, then maybe we were. I may be green, but I've got more sense than to fall for a clever line from someone like you who—who admits to having a string of girl friends who wear his bikinis and . . . and . . ."

He lifted a quizzical brow. "And?"

"And who admits to not believing in love, but only in lust!" she flashed triumphantly.

He pursed his lips and studied a callus in the palm of his hand. "What would you say if I told you I'd changed my mind about love?"

Thunder rumbled sullenly in the distance and Lacy caught her breath. From under the cover of her long lashes she studied him suspiciously. "I'd say you'd been turned down in your cold-blooded proposal and were trying to build up your ego again by handing out a whopping big line to the first girl you came across," she said firmly, and before he could utter a denial—if he had the nerve to even try—she continued. "So I'll put it into plain English for you—go peddle your line somewhere else. It won't wash with me. There's one thing I learned early in my life and that's not to be taken in by . . . by physical pressures. Some things just aren't worth the . . . the pleasures of a few . . . of a few moments," she floundered.

He was studying her openly now and Lacy squirmed under his speculative gaze. Perhaps she could have worded that a little differently. He seemed to think she had learned it firsthand instead of from the example set by her own parents. But what if he did?

Her chin lifted fractionally and she returned his look as boldly as she dared. Did it matter what reason she had for resisting his advances as long as she *did* resist them? If he ever discovered how vulnerable she was to him, he'd have an open field and she'd end up—no, the result didn't bear thinking about. There were too many possible ramifications, the very least of which was a broken heart.

"Well?" he probed gently. "I'd be curious to know what was behind that remarkable display of expressions that's been parading across your face. You'll never make a successful secret agent, Lacy."

Chapter Eight

The sight of the enormous white cruise ship several hours later made Lacy wonder just how far they had sailed. Far enough to reach the shipping lanes, obviously, but in which direction? And to what ends? If it were simply a means of making her beg, then Jordan would have a long wait. She might be short a good many qualities, but pure stubbornness was not among them!

Yesterday's sunburn had faded to a rosy brown and for lack of something better to do she climbed up on top of the cabin and spread herself out on one of his bath sheets. The tanning oil she had found among his toiletries was just that, a tan promoter rather than a screen, but it would be better than nothing. She annointed herself liberally, making a conscious effort to avoid looking aft, to where Jordan leaned back at the controls, perfectly at ease with his conscience after deliberately kidnapping a citizen of the United States of America!

She had eaten very little of the breakfast he had prepared and none of the lunch and now she was beginning to regret it. There was no real point in being childish about the thing, she rationalized. Jordan was being childish enough for both of them in simply ignoring her protests and sailing away with her to lord knew where or to what purpose.

After dozing in the sun and waking to worry over the nagging questions in her mind, Lacy rolled over and untied the strings of the green bikini to allow the sun to do its job with no interference. She'd be headed home, as soon as Jordan came to his senses, with a badly bruised heart and some unforgettable memories. Might as well take home the appearance, at least, of a splendid Caribbean holiday. It might obviate the need for explaining her long stay to Aunt Lottie.

A slight change in course brought the boom swinging across and the sun was now filtered through the billowing white sail. Jordan had come about with the finesse he showed in most matters so that there had not been even the faintest jolt. She frowned at the lack of something concrete to complain of.

The man did everything with skill and grace, darn it! Even to the point of kidnapping her with all the aplomb of someone taking her out for a pleasant afternoon's sail. Oh, she had no doubt that he'd return her eventually, but for now she was helpless. She had pleaded with him to allow her to go ashore at Cancún and start the proceedings that would allow her to get back into the States. She had promised to repay any out-of-pocket expenses, had explained that she'd be terrible company for him if he was simply looking for a playmate, and finally she had berated him for being so cruel.

To which he had responded by offering her a glass of

white wine and a ceviche he had begged from the chef
aboard the *Star*. "Excellent stuff! He marinates it with
lime and freshly pressed olive oil and has the onions
flown in from a little place in Georgia."

It had been at that point that she had slammed
herself into her cabin and alternately glowered and
moped until she had fallen into a light sleep. And now
she had dozed away even more time out here under the
sails. Wasn't sleep supposed to be some sort of an
escape mechanism? A symptom of depression?

But was it really depression that made her skin tingle
and the nerves along her spine register the presence of
the man behind her as clearly as if she were facing him
instead of coiled up here with her back to him?

"No breakfast, no lunch—aren't you ready for high
tea by now?" he queried, having come silently up
behind her.

"I had breakfast, thank you," Lacy grumbled even as
her stomach leapt in anticipation.

"Correction—you drank two thirds a cup of coffee
and took one bite of toast before throwing your dishes
aside and stalking out in a high dudgeon." He knelt
beside her, his thin khakis straining at the thighs, and
offered her two thick slabs of brown bread with tantalizing bits and pieces sticking out from between the
crusts.

Perversely, she insisted she was not hungry and he
placed the offering against a hatch cover for safe-
keeping and dropped down beside her. "You're really
being pretty silly about this whole thing, you know, but
if you want to go on a hunger strike, that's up to you.
At least you won't have much to render unto Neptune
when the squall hits us."

She looked at him then, alarm at his words giving
way to alarm of a different sort when she saw his face at

close range. The crinkles around his intensely blue eyes were in full evidence and she could see the shadow of amusement in his clear gaze. "What squall?"

"You've been so determined not to look at me you missed the pile-up of clouds that's been following us for the past few hours. I don't think we'll be able to outrun it—the wind will probably drop to nothing just before it strikes, so we'll just come about and head up to ride it out. Meanwhile, I thought you'd be better off for something to tide you over till dinner."

Her eyes strayed unwillingly to the thick, meaty sandwich and she gave in. By the time she had picked the last crumb from the napkin and finished the chilled wine, she felt immeasurably better.

"Where are we?" she asked.

Very carefully Jordan took the large paper napkin from her and blotted the corner of her mouth before telling her that they were no more than a few miles from both Isla Mujeres and Cancún.

"I thought it was knots when one was on water," she threw out while her mind was busy with the little she knew of the coast of Quintana Roo. They had been sailing for ages and had got nowhere evidently!

"The knot is a measure of speed, not distance." His finger lifted one of the straps of her bikini bra and she realized she had forgotten to retie it. She snatched it away from him and he grinned as he watched her snarl it in her hair in an effort to tie it behind her neck. Finally, he took the two ends from her and she turned her back to allow him better access.

She felt the brush of his fingers on the burning skin of her back and the flimsy scrap of material fell to her lap. Gasping, she wrapped her arms around her breasts and turned to glare at him. "Jordan, I warned you—I'm not going to play your games. You've got the wrong girl for that sort of affair!"

"Have I?" he drawled easily, leaning back to survey her from narrowed eyes. "I don't think so."

A cat's paw of wind blew fitfully across the deck and she grabbed for the bra before it went over the side. "Leave me alone!" she said grimly.

"Or?"

"What do you mean, or?" she repeated sullenly.

"Or what do you propose to do?" he challenged, reminding her all over again of her vulnerable position.

"I hardly think you'd resort to brute force," she muttered. "It can't do your ego any good to be turned down by one woman and then be rejected by another when you want to salve your wounded macho pride. Surely you'd rather have a . . . a willing partner than someone you'd have to force." She was struggling to fasten her bra and when Jordan reached out as if to help her she slapped his hand away.

Moving swiftly, he caught at her hand and pressed it slowly away from her body, so that the tiny scrap of sea green jersey hung like a limp flag from the fingers of her other hand, covering little at all of her body. The line of demarcation where rosy tan gave way to milk white stood out plainly and Lacy twisted furiously to escape the steely manacle. "Leave . . . me . . . *alone!*" she seethed. Her eyes glistened widely with anger, fear, and something else that seemed to thrum through the charged atmosphere between them.

"Force?" Jordan suggested softly, drawing her inexorably closer to where he sat crosslegged slightly behind her. "I think we both know just about how much force would be involved if . . . when . . . I decide to take you."

A cold feeling of weakness washed swiftly through her. "Jordan, you wouldn't . . ."

"Make you? No. You've hinted at something in your past—I'm not asking for any confidences, but believe me, this time it won't be an experience you look back on with repugnance." He had drawn her so far off balance by now that only by the merest thread did she hold herself away. They were so close together that she could feel the heat of his body and it contrasted vividly with the growing chill of the ocean breeze. Overhead the sails strained tautly against the aluminum mast and the sheets, and the wind whistled through the standing rigging.

Her surrender was signaled by a movement of less than an inch—she allowed her shoulder to come to rest against his chest and then both his arms closed around her as she shut her mind to the consequences of her action. "This is hardly the time or the place," he whispered as his mouth moved from one eyelid to the other, settling only momentarily to brush over her thick lashes. "But who am I to refuse such a charming capitulation?" He removed the scrap of cloth from her nerveless fingers and tossed it over the side.

"Jordan!" she wailed.

His lips trailed down her throat, sweet from the scented tanning oil, and slowed as they neared the crest of the snowy mound below. "From now on, you'll swim my way," he taunted just before capturing a small nipple with strong white teeth. He tugged gently and the pain was transmuted into a throbbing pleasure that swept through her body like molten lava, gathering in crevasses to smolder into flames.

Her hands found naked skin between belt and shirt and she insinuated them under the cotton knit until, with an impatient oath, he lifted himself and tore the shirt over his head, sending it flying to catch around a shroud and flap in the growing breeze. "Now . . . touch me. I want your hands to know my body as intimately as mine will know yours," he growled, leading the way with an exploration of his own, an exploration that the small bit of clothing left her did little to detain.

There was scarcely room to move among the clutter of cleated halyard, mast, hatch cover, and running lights, and when Jordan's weight pressed her thigh down aginst the low railing that ran around the cabin's edges she caught her breath.

"What is it, darling?" he lifted his head to smile down at her and she was stunned—stunned and excited by what she saw there. Gone was the brilliant blue of his eyes. Against heavy lids, the darkness of passion had swallowed up the color except for a tiny rim, and there was a forcefulness about the chin and mouth that told her Jordan was exerting tremendous strength to control his emotions. Her abdomen quivered as the breath fluttered shallowly in her lungs and his eyes moved relentlessly to follow the imperceptible motion, leaving a trail of fire in their wake.

He buried his face in her trembling flesh and she doubled up around his head, moaning against the overwhelming desire that held her like a leaf in a hurricane, tossing her to a sure destruction.

Suddenly the sloop lurched wildly as the boom swung across the cockpit and Jordan was on his feet in an instant, leaving Lacy lying in sprawled abandon beneath him. "Not now!" he muttered, shooting her a single intense glance before leaping into the cockpit to adjust to the inadvertent gibe.

By the time she followed him into the cockpit Lacy was wearing Jordan's shirt over her bikini pants and she paused only long enough to ask if he needed help before darting below to the sanctuary of her cabin. Not even the wallowing of the small sloop in the steadily increasing seas pushed out the consciousness of the narrow escape she had had.

* * *

By the time the clouds had blocked out all vestiges of daylight the wind had dropped and a sullen rain had commenced. Lacy had spent the intervening hours huddled on her bunk, alternately afraid Jordan would seek her there and afraid he wouldn't. Finally, it was sheer curiosity that drove her out into the main cabin.

It was empty, but the glowing lights on the assortment of electronic navigational aids and radios made her pause and wish she had paid more attention to the operation of them on the cruise from Belize to Isla Mujeres.

On the other hand, who could she call? The Coast Guard? Mayday? She'd feel like all sorts of fool having to report that the man she had lived with aboard the sloop for the past few weeks had suddenly become a kidnapper.

Which left only one alternative—to go along with him until he tired of her and then . . . Hope for the best, she supposed dolefully, which was no hope at all.

Jordan came below in a sudden flurry of raindrops and cool air. He had not bothered with foul weather gear and now his wet clothes clung to his body with embarrassing faithfulness. Catching her gaze on him, he shot her a warm, crinkly grin. "Hello, love—been keeping out of trouble?" Before she could manage a reply, he continued with a weather prognosis. "Looks as if we might be in for more of the same over the next few hours. A line of squalls stretching from Guatemala to the Gulf Coast moving northeastward. Can't outrun them—that's certain—and I want to be well away from the reef, so we'll just lay offshore here and duck back outside in the morning."

Half suspecting he was only trying to frighten her, she tilted her head and cast him a sidelong glance.

138

"What reef? And anyway, it can't be all that dangerous —I saw that cruise ship, you know."

"Distances can be deceiving on water. The ship was outside the reef, in the Outer Channel—bound for Cozumel, probably, and points south. We'll stay here in the Inner Channel until daylight and then cast off again, barring trouble." He was leaning over the console, making minute adjustments in the VHF. A confusion of noise filled the cabin, discouraging any further questions on her part. It was not until she gave up and moved to the small gimbaled stove that he nodded his satisfaction and adjusted the squelch so that a blessed quietness descended over them once more.

"I could do with some coffee if you're making," he remarked, using a linen tea towel to blot his face and neck.

"Are you hungry?"

He was. So was she, and the next hour passed peacefully enough as they moved about the cramped quarters preparing a meal. If Lacy was at pains to avoid physical contact, then it appeared that Jordan was no less anxious. Both of them were careful to mention nothing of Lacy's plight, but as she cleaned up the last of the ceviche left over from lunch, she mulled over her situation and tried to assure herself that Jordan was only playing another game with her—that he fully intended to take her to Cancún once he had tired of his fun.

At any rate, she wouldn't give him the satisfaction of revealing her anxiety. Perhaps if he thought she was going to cling to him like a limpet, he might change his mind and release her willingly. For all he had seemingly been rejected by one woman, she had an idea that women threw themselves at him with boring regularity. He had everything any woman could possibly want, and well he must know it.

Putting away the clean, dry dishes, Lacy became aware of Jordan's presence behind her. She stiffened warily and against her will the blood began to race through her veins.

"Darling?" he said huskily, as one warm, hard hand came down on her shoulder.

Fighting against her own traitorous responses in the only way she knew how, she turned on him. "Don't you 'darling' me! Look, just because you have a captive audience for your talented performance as a—a great lover, don't think I'm taken in for one minute! If you think I'm going to ruin the rest of my life just for a fling with some seagoing playboy, you're sadly mistaken! I may be green, but I'm not stupid!"

The hand had fallen away and Jordan returned her fiery accusations with a bleak sort of calm that made her close her mouth abruptly. Her conscience whispered that he had not led her anywhere she hadn't been more than willing to follow and she ordered it to be quiet. She didn't need any oversentimental conscience tipping the scales in Jordan's favor—not when every cell in her body was crying out to her to take whatever he offered, however fleeting, and live for the moment.

In the exaggerated silence that spun out between them Lacy was barely aware of the creak and wail of the wind in the rigging, of the hard rain that beat against the portholes in fitful gusts. Her legs automatically adjusted to the movement of the hull, and the longer the silence lasted, the more impossible it became to break.

It was a peculiar sound from outside, along with an almost imperceptible jolt, that shattered the tension. Jordan immediately assumed a listening attitude and then, without a word, he was out the hatch, leaving it to swing open behind him. Lacy stood frozen for several long moments before the clatter of the swinging door and the rain pouring in roused her from her stillness. She darted across the cabin and up the steps to poke her head outside, remembering that Jordan had slipped off his sodden deck shoes during the meal and was out there in the darkness moving around a slick deck in his bare feet.

For all she knew there was no danger, but the very idea of his slipping overboard was unbearable. "Jordan!" she shrieked over the whine of wind and the drumming of rain.

"Get back inside!" he yelled immediately.

"What's the trouble?"

"Nothing I can't handle! The darned jerry-rigged— get below!" he bellowed, leaving her to wonder if they were in dire danger of sinking before the night was out.

Headed into the wind with only the staysail flying, they had been relatively steady, but now it seemed as if the wind came at them from all sides. There was no way of knowing what was going on outside, for the sound of the storm covered Jordan's movements overhead and Lacy's imagination grew more and more fevered until the hatch suddenly flew open and he took the three steps in a single stride. Without sparing her so much as a glance, he opened the tool locker and disappeared topside with an assortment of handtools.

Searching for an excuse to join him on deck, Lacy muttered suddenly and then leapt up and began scrabbling through a drawer in search of a flashlight. If he were going to be washed overboard, she was darned well going to be ready to throw him a life preserver! Pausing only long enough to hook the door to after her, she scanned the darkly gleaming wetness until she caught sight of Jordan's ghostlike figure bent over something near the shroud on the port side. Clinging to the handrail, she eased her way along before switching on the flashlight.

Without lifting his head, he barked out, "Here! To the left a little—that's it! Hold it now for just a minute!"

Within five minutes she was as soaked as he was, and after only a few minutes more she was shivering in spite of the comparative warmth of the tropical storm. Her blood had seemingly thinned rapidly during the weeks she had been in the Caribbean.

"Hold it steady, can't you?"

"Sorry."

He sighed and straightened up, yanking on the stainless steel cable experimentally. "No, sweetheart, I'm sorry. You shouldn't be out here in the first place. I could have managed."

Turning to make her way back into the safety of the cockpit, with Jordan following, Lacy remained silent. While she hadn't expected to be thanked profusely for her efforts—she supposed that holding a flashlight couldn't be called a heroic measure—she hadn't expected to have them dismissed as worthless. "I was just curious, that's all," she tossed over her shoulder.

"It'll make a tale for your grandchildren, right?" Jordan mocked as he ushered her inside.

Without turning to look at him, she lifted a disdainful shoulder. "I'll have forgotten all about the whole thing long before then," she dismissed. A tremor passed over her and she dropped the flashlight in the drawer and closed it. Still she did not turn to face him.

"Will you?" The odd inflection in his voice caused her chin to lift fractionally and she wondered if he had any idea just how worried she had been for his safety. The whole darned sailboat could have foundered and she wouldn't have looked twice, but if Jordan had been injured trying to rig repairs alone on a wet, windy night—worse still, been washed overboard—she'd have died!

"I'll mix toddies—we've earned it," he said gruffly, moving around her to reach in the liquor compartment.

"None for me, thanks," she declined. "I think I'll turn in. Uh . . . we *will* be going in to Cancún in the morning, won't we?" It was a stab in the dark and she paused in the companionway for his answer, dreading the very thing she sought.

"Now what gave you that idea?"

"Jordan, you've *had* your fun! Now give up! You can't keep me here against my will. It's . . . it's criminal!"

"Then if I'm to be charged with one capital offense, why not two?"

This time she turned to face him, and at the sight of the low fire simmering in his eyes she was sorry she hadn't simply run for cover while she had the chance. Held captive by the sheer force of his personality, Lacy was easy prey for the large predator who stalked her so effortlessly. With one slow, almost indolent gesture, Jordan pulled her against him, their wet bodies quickly warming from the contact, and when he lowered his face to hers, she accepted his kiss with a fatalism that bordered on relief.

All thoughts of escape forgotten, Lacy allowed herself to respond to his deliberate caresses until, with an inarticulate cry, she reached up and pulled his teasing mouth down again to hers. Butterfly kisses on her eyes, her cheeks, the corners of her lips had only whetted her appetite for something more and the appetite grew voraciously as Jordan allowed himself the freely offered access to her mouth.

Quickly, his hands found the chilled hardness of her

nipples and manipulated them to his own desires until she twisted restlessly against him, striving for a closeness beyond any she had known before. It was as if the storm that blotted out the sight of land also erased all memories of land-learned lessons. The past never was—the future not to be considered. There was only the essence of this moment, with the reality of Jordan's hands moving over her body with a sureness that tapped the deepest stores of her womanhood, sending fresh surges of desire to the surface again and again.

His cabin was only a few steps away and he simply swept her up and moved forward with unerring instincts in the darkened passageway. With no word spoken between them, he lowered her onto his bed, and when she reached for him, he paused only long enough to rip off his sodden clothes before joining her.

"You're cold," he growled against her hair. The rain had drawn her curls up into a damp, springy soap-and-sun-scented mass and he buried his face in it as his hands began easing the wet shirt from her shoulders. Any coldness was only skin deep; inside, her metabolism soared as the fierce demands of her body blocked out all other considerations.

At the sudden realization that there was nothing at all between the n, Lacy stiffened. It was only a momentary reaction, born of her knowledge that soon she'd be taking an irreversible step. Virginity was not renewable. Once he had made her his, she'd never again be the same Lacy Davis, and even though the possibility of a child's resulting from one night of love was negligible, did she dare risk it?

"Ahhhh," she breathed in an audible sigh as Jordan trailed a tantalizing hand up the velvety skin of her inner thigh. Had she any real choice? She loved this man. If he wanted her, she knew she'd never be able to deny him—to deny herself this once-in-a-lifetime pleasure that was rapidly growing into a compulsion she hadn't the strength to deny.

His hands burned teasing circles on her abdomen and she moved involuntarily, seeking his touch with an instinct she hardly recognized. Words screamed silently inside her head, words of love that she dared not utter. One word could halt the compelling drive of his passion and she was too far gone to risk it, but oh! how she ached for a reassuring sign.

The hot, moist path of his tongue on her flesh brought a series of shudders to her, and when she felt his weight come upon her, she stiffened in spite of herself, her eyes first widening and then closing.

"What is it, love?" he whispered. "Don't stop me now, darling. I'll be good to us both."

"I—Jordan . . ." The words burst from her with no conscious thought. "Don't hurt me."

For a moment she thought he hadn't heard her. Her words had been only a breath against the sound of the diminishing storm outside, balanced precariously against the growing tempest in the small, dark cabin.

"Lacy . . ." The uneven rasp of his voice registered dimly over the sound of her thundering heart, her gasping breath. "Lacy, you have . . . ah . . . done this before, haven't you?"

The suspicion dawned in his voice even as he spoke and she reached for him to pull him back into the mindless world of the senses, but he wasn't to be denied. "Lacy . . . Woman, don't tell me you're a virgin! Not now!"

Allowing her hands to drop from his neck as he lifted himself from her, she sighed. "Does it matter so much? There—there has to be a first time for everything." Her desperate attempt at flippancy failed miserably and she rolled over to curl up against the emptiness. The warmth of his body removed, she felt colder than ever.

"Just tell me one thing," he grated. "What the devil was the point of all those cute tales you spun me about your lurid past?"

"I didn't tell you anything!" she charged angrily. She felt rejected and that hurt.

"Not in so many words," he said tiredly, slamming through a drawer in search of dry clothing. "Just a bit of teasing here and there with a breathless retreat behind the painful past in case the going got too hot and heavy for you. Is that the way you get your kicks, Lacy? The old shell game—now you see it, now you don't?" His contempt poured over her in blistering waves, magnified a thousand times by her own self-condemnation.

In a voice devoid of all emotion she reminded him that it had been he who had rejected her instead of the other way around.

"Believe it or not, I draw the line at seducing virgins—even those who play dangerous games by leading a man on and then turning him off with some melodramatic hint about the past. Well, keep your secrets, little girl! Just try to stay out of my way from now on, will you?"

When she would have stopped him, he hushed her protests with one rude word. "Stay here if you want to. I'll be on deck. At least I know how to fight against the weather!"

In the end Lacy returned to her own cabin—not that it did her much good. For hours she rolled and twisted, staring into the darkness as she went over in her mind every encounter with Jordan from the very first. Had she actually told him it was her own past that had ruined her for casual encounters? She couldn't be certain—she rather recalled a decision to allow him to think as much. At the time she must have had a reason, but now, in the face of his total rejection of her, she wished she had been more honest with him. It was just that she had so few weapons in her arsenal when it came to fighting the attractions of a man like Jordan— especially when she wanted nothing more then to lose the battle.

Only hours earlier she had told him she might be green but she wasn't stupid—then she had to go and prove herself to be the stupidest creature alive! He'd probably be dropping her off at Cancún at first light and thanking providence to be rid of her. If only she had been frank with him from the first, they might at least have parted on good terms.

It was not the sight of Cancún's gleaming white hotels that greeted her when she came topside the next morning, however. There, covering a low, sandy island, was one of the most spectacular sights she could have imagined—acres and acres of rosy flamingos, like a noisy pink sea. Even as she watched, groups of them lifted into the air to circle over the others until the air was filled with brilliant clouds of the long-necked birds, and then, as if on a hidden signal, they swerved and headed out over the water.

Lacy's mouth hung open in astonished admiration. She caught a glimpse of the brilliant reflection on the purplish water in the distance and then her eyes were captured by pink feathers drifting on the clear aquamarine water immediately beneath them. Becoming slowly aware of Jordan's presence just behind her, she swung her head around and in doing so caught sight of a familiar blue and green catamaran.

"Pepe," she murmured to herself, and at that moment, from the other side of the *Phoenix*, came a cheerful greeting that seemed to shrivel her on the spot.

"Hi! Jordie! Where'd you get to, anyway? We thought you'd been caught in the squall and decided to lay over at Cancún," Lolene called gaily. "Give me a hand and I'll join you. We can . . ." Her slightly husky drawl faded out as she came alongside in the launch and caught sight of Lacy across the cockpit.

The two women stared at each other with a mixture of dismay and animosity—both emotions mutual. Jordan stepped smoothly into the breech.

"We took a spin outside and then laid over off Puerta Juárez last night. Sorry if you were worried. I expected to be back yesterday morning." He offered no explanation of the delay, and Lacy, after one look at the grim set of his jaw, doubted that Lolene would dare pursue the matter. If so, the golden-tanned blonde had more nerve than she herself. In spite of a burning curiosity about Jordan's strange behavior, she'd rather stick her head in a lion's mouth than question him about his intentions.

Chapter Nine

The occupants of the *Star*'s launch—Naylor, Tad, Jenny, and Lolene—came aboard for breakfast at Jordan's invitation, bringing with them the rather elaborate picnic meal they had packed. Jenny and Lacy had the task of making coffee and setting out the feast for a group that more or less filled the cabin, and Lacy found herself sharing a bench with Naylor after pouring coffee for everyone.

"I don't mind telling you, dollface, you had a certain blonde, who shall be nameless, in a bobtailed tizzy," he whispered facetiously while Tad and Jordan compared storm notes.

"Sorry." Glad of an excuse to keep from elaborating, she took an enormous bite of one of the delectable pastries baked by the *Star*'s chef. Jordan was telling Tad about splicing something to the something-or-other that had been jerry-rigged in Belize City and they both deplored the dearth of decent repair shops in that particular area. Tilting her head to drain her coffee cup, she became aware of Lolene's speculative gaze on her and Lolene asked if she had gotten her tourist card yet.

"Not yet." Lacy cut her eyes at Jordan and was immediately squelched by the message she read there.

Lolene persisted. "But surely the papers must be here by now. It's been ages since you sent for them and express service doesn't take that long, even this far off the beaten track. Naylor"—Lolene turned to the man sitting uncomfortably close to Lacy—"darling, can't you *do* something for the poor child? Call someone—call the Embassy."

Jenny Wainwright leaned forward. "Oh, that reminds me, Lacy, you left your bag on board the launch. Say—I never heard what actually happened that night. Someone said you'd gone in the second launch and we thought you'd gone back to the *Phoenix* and turned in, so you can imagine how worried we were when Jordan came climbing up the side demanding to know what we'd done with you."

It was almost worth the discomfort just to see the subtle shadings of expression among the small group, Lacy decided. Jenny's friendly curiosity was mirrored to a lesser degree in Tad's face, but Lolene looked as if she could wring Jenny's neck for broaching the subject, and Jordan—oddly enough, Jordan looked almost embarrassed.

It was Naylor who changed the subject. Once more it occurred to Lacy that the older man thoroughly enjoyed the game of observing the interplay between the people in his company and was not above acting as a bit of a catalyst should it prove entertaining—though in this instance no prod from him had been needed.

There was a sound of splashing outside and Lacy

turned to see the rubber raft bearing Pepe de Palanco approach from astern.

"*Hola!* I see you found the missing passenger, Señor Stone," he greeted them cheerfully, backpaddling in order to hold the raft out so that he could see Jordan, looking deceptively relaxed by the open hatch.

Lacy, glad of the distraction, returned the young Mexican's gleaming smile with an eager one of her own, inviting him to come aboard for coffee and pastries.

Pepe looked quickly to Jordan and, at the curt nod of reinforcement, made fast his rubber raft and swung lithely into the cockpit.

The others wandered outside and soon were distributed around, some on the comfortable lockers and some on top of the cabin. Pepe made room for himself beside Lacy and each of them leaned a shoulder against the base of the aluminum mast. He began telling her in a low undertone about his worries for her when Jordan had accosted him on the night of her disappearance.

"He seemed to think I had spirited you away. I half expected to have him demand to search my *Felicia*, but when I offered the use of my uncle's truck, he seemed satisfied at my innocence in the matter." He leaned closer and Lacy was conscious of the rather flowery scent of his cologne. "I would have preferred *not* to be so innocent, but with a—what do you say—a tough customer like your Señor Stone breathing fire, perhaps it's as well you turned me down."

Demurely wide eyed, Lacy said, "Oh? I didn't even know you'd made me an offer."

They grinned in easy understanding. Nationality notwithstanding, Pepe was a type she understood from her recent college days. He grimaced slightly and she looked around to see Naylor seating himself on her other side, a speculative look in his tired eyes.

"Do I understand correctly that you've decided to . . . uh . . . prolong your vacation, Lacy? Then perhaps I can encourage you to visit aboard the *Star* for a while. I'm sure we can work out a"—he pursed his lips as a slow gleam appeared in the watery brown eyes—"an arrangement with Stone and Lolene. We can offer much more in the way of entertainment aboard the *Star*—all sorts of entertainment."

Lacy edged away from the middle-aged man, a movement that brought her much closer to Pepe, who looked on with unconcealed interest. Something about the man made her shrink in revulsion—something more than the flabby browned flesh that hung over his white shorts and the lecherous speculation he didn't bother to hide. It was as if his very mind offended her.

"I don't think I'll be around much longer," she began when Jordan moved up to where they were sitting. He was still standing in the cockpit and his eyes were more or less level with Lacy's, but it was impossible to read them.

"I understand Horace and Daphne are flying down to join you aboard the *Star* tonight. That makes a pretty full house, doesn't it?" He was speaking to Naylor, but Lacy was aware of his gaze on her, even so.

"Not at all, not at all," Naylor assured him urbanely. "Gus flew the others back to Cancún yesterday—the Sponsons and Dudleys are going to hop across to Acapulco for a week or so before heading home. I've got plenty of room for everyone, so why not take a break from that bathtub toy of yours? Glad to have both of you—the boy, too, if he'd care to come along," he added with a perfunctory jab of his thumb toward Pepe.

Lacy, incensed on Pepe's behalf at the condescending invitation, assumed that Horace and Daphne were Tad and Lolene's parents. She had no desire to meet them, much less to be forced to socialize with them aboard the *Star*. She sought Jordan's eyes to send him a silent message to that effect, but with a feeling of miserable disbelief she heard him accepting Naylor's offer.

With the flamingos dispersed, they lazed around off the low lying islands that were home to thousands of assorted birds. While the three crafts drifted gently over the glassy swells, Lacy and Jenny swam, and were soon joined by Tad and Pepe. Lacy tried not to be aware of Jordan, Naylor, and Lolene relaxing in perfect amiability aboard the *Phoenix*. The plans were to remain in the Contoy, or Bird Island vicinity, where Naylor had made arrangements for one of the native guides to provide them with freshly caught barracuda, barbecued island style, and perhaps lobster and the traditional Macum fish soup, then cruise back to Isla Mujeres late in the afternoon to enjoy the spectacular tropical sunset.

The *Morningstar* launch sported a pink and white canopy, but the company seemed to prefer the comparatively spartan accommodations of the *Phoenix* and Lacy was grateful to take advantage of Pepe's uncomplicated companionship. It seemed impossible to even move about the sloop without stumbling over Lolene and Jordan, and she found that her own cabin had been more or less taken over by the women from the *Star*.

During the course of the seemingly endless day, Lacy discovered that Tad, at least, was looking forward to meeting his father and stepmother. It seemed that Jordan had always been a sort of buffer between the older MacArthur and his irresponsible son and Tad was counting on Jordan to plead his case again—the case this time being an engagement with Jenny Wainright instead of the girl his father had picked out for him.

Wistfully, Lacy wondered if Jordan would take the

opportunity to plead his own case as well. What was it Jenny had said about the pair of them? That Jordan and Lolene had belonged to each other since they had cut their teeth on the same playpen? He might be chafing at the bit now, but he'd settle down soon enough. From the sound of things it was a foregone conclusion, the merging of the two families that had once been joined in a business venture. She didn't even know what line of business the MacArthurs were in, but it wouldn't be any penny-ante game, she'd be willing to bet. And Jordan moved in the same rarefied atmosphere—too rich for Lacy's peasant blood by a long shot! The sooner she got away, the sooner she'd be able to breath comfortably.

The dinner, served on the island under a thatched roof, was delectable, but Lacy couldn't enjoy it. For one thing, she had eaten barracuda the night her stomach had rebelled and so she didn't quite trust it despite the fact that it was better than any fish she had ever tasted. She picked at the lobster and tried the soup, but as the evening wore on she became more and more miserable.

She dreaded having to go along with the others aboard the *Star* and meet Lolene's parents and she hated having to sit here and watch the self-assured blonde juggle the two older men with a skill born of long practice. Even Pepe seemed to have fallen prey to her physical beauty and her biting sense of humor.

At least Lacy wasn't the butt of her malicious comments. Her stepmother, Daphne, came in for the bulk of them. Lacy felt sorry for any woman who was forced by marriage into close relationship with the sharp-tongued girl. She wondered how Jenny could even contemplate it, but then, perhaps, it was different if you were born into that stratum of society. Jenny's father owned an airline.

As the group prepared to leave the island and return to Isla Mujeres by their various vessels, Lacy, seeing Lolene board the *Phoenix*, turned to Pepe, who was wading out with his rubber raft. "How about a passenger? Looks like Jordan's already picked his crew."

She didn't care for the brief glimmer of sympathy she saw in the young Mexican's eyes, but it was preferable to being odd man out on board the *Phoenix* for the next few hours.

Naylor, preparing to board the *Star*'s launch, quickly covered a flicker of displeasure, allowing a measuring glance to touch the two sailboats. Then he called to Tad and Jenny to join him and announced that he'd see the others later on board the *Star*. "I assume you'll be coming in under sail—far more romantic under the circumstances." The sneer in his voice was hardly discernible.

The launch bobbed lightly between the sloop and the catamaran and across the intervening space Lacy could feel Jordan's penetrating gaze. Suddenly she was sick and tired of all the subtle undertones of tension, at the way Jordan was frowning at her, the way Lolene was devouring him with her eyes, and the way Naylor was studying them all. She wanted nothing more than to go back home, where life was uncomplicated and the games people played were gin rummy and canasta. Her nerves had had about all they could stand in the past few days!

A sunset, viewed alone from the deck of a sailboat as it glided silently through warm, transparent waters, was the best tranquilizer she could have found. By the time Pepe joined her, dropping down beside her with an undemanding smile, she felt almost up to the ordeal ahead. As long as she could maintain her objectivity by reminding herself that the lives of these people didn't *really* impinge on hers, it only *seemed* that way, she'd come through unscathed.

Ahead of them and off to one side, the *Phoenix* came about on a tack that would take them even further away. The *Felicia*, lighter weight, could probably have overtaken them easily, but Pepe seemed in no hurry and certainly Lacy wasn't.

"I think you're going to be taking home a souvenir even more painful than your sunburned nose," Pepe suggested sympathetically.

When Lacy questioned him with a look, he said softly, "Your very sore little heart, hmmm? It will take longer to heal, but in the long run you'll recover. Take it from a man who's suffered many broken hearts." His half-derisive tone invited her to share his amusement. He had told her before of his many conquests and now he offered the commiseration of a fellow sufferer.

"I don't stand much of a chance, do I?" she laughed with painful honesty.

He shrugged with Latin exaggeration. "If it were me you'd have every chance in the world, but then I like a warm-blooded woman, not one who can wither a man like a killing frost with one glance from icy eyes. Perhaps Señor Stone will tire of having to protect himself against frostbite and turn to someone more . . ." He finished the statement with a flattering gesture of expressive hands and Lacy laughed, not at all convinced but enormously comforted.

Lacy was forced to board the *Phoenix* once they reached the harbor at Isla Mujeres. She needed to shower off the day's accumulation of salt water and suntan oil, and her clothes, such as they were, were still in her quarters. It was a relief to find no sign of Lolene when she came below, at least. She could hear Jordan in his own cabin and she slipped quietly into her room and closed the door.

It was impossible to avoid him. With only the one head and two berths, they had to pass each other half a dozen times in the process of getting dressed for dinner aboard the *Star*.

She tried to beg off, knowing all the while it would do no good. "Jordan, why don't I just stay here tonight? It isn't as if I knew these people, and frankly, except for Jenny and maybe Tad, I don't like your other friends. I feel like a hypocrite accepting Naylor's hospitality when the very thought of him gives me the creeps."

"Hold that thought," he laughed, fishing a dry pair of deck shoes from a locker. "Maybe I need you around to give me moral support."

She leaned in the opening of her door, brushing her damp hair. "Your morals might need supporting, but I'd hardly be of any use to you," she pointed out sarcastically.

One lifted eyebrow revealed a speculative gleam in his blue eyes. "Are you throwing out another teaser about your immoral past? I thought I'd taught you better than that."

In spite of the warm color that rose uncomfortably to her face, she didn't turn away. "I offered to tell you about my past once and you didn't care to listen."

He stared at her disbelievingly. "When?"

"Not so long ago." She shrugged. "I don't remember just when. Does it matter?"

"It matters when you pick a totally impossible time like this to bring up the matter. In case I haven't mentioned it, girl, your sense of timing is deplorable."

Her fingers were busy attempting to braid her hair before piling it on top of her head and she muttered impatiently, covering her embarrassment in the activity.

"Let it hang loose," he ordered, coming to stand beside her in the close confines of the companionway.

"What . . . ? Oh, you mean my hair."

"Take it any way you want," he said gruffly, and reached out to undo the work her hands had done. "You look lovely tonight, Lacy."

Staring intensely at the bottom button on his black cotton shirt, Lacy muttered an embarrassed thanks. He had bought and paid for her dress after all—he should approve of it. "I still wish I didn't have to go," she insisted.

Placing a hand on each side of her face, Jordan tilted it so that he could smile down at her chidingly. "It never occurred to me that you were a coward, Lacy Davis. Besides, you'll like Daphne. And we won't stay too late. I have a matter to clear up with Horace and then, I promise you, we'll leave."

With compunction she began to apologize. "Jordan, I don't mean to be rude—really. There's no reason for you to have to leave your friends. I can paddle—"

"Your own canoe?" he finshed for her, still holding her captive with his eyes and his hands.

"Well, *your* own canoe, at any rate," she conceded with a small laugh.

"That's better. Now," he announced with a firm tone, "there's something I want you to keep in mind until we can get a few things straight."

"What is it?"

"This," he said softly, lowering his mouth to hers with a quick, hard pressure. He released her then and turned away to switch on the mooring lights.

Jordan was right about one thing. She did like Daphne MacArthur. The small, round woman with her cropped brassy curls was as different from her elegant stepdaughter as night from day, and she made no bones about the fact that she had been an entertainer before she lost her figure.

"I was always hungry in those days," she giggled, "so I guess it's Horace's fault for feeding me so well."

The company seemed to separate into small clumps, with Jordan going off with Horace and Tad immediately after dinner, leaving Naylor to entertain the women. Pepe seemed slightly overawed by the splendor of the yacht, and when Jenny offered to show him around, he agreed with alacrity. Naylor brought over drinks for the three remaining women and then he and Lolene drifted away to talk in low undertones, leaving Lacy with Daphne MacArthur.

The bouncy blonde chattered nonstop about matters concerning both her stepchildren and her husband, and Lacy soon learned far more than she wanted to about Horace's dyspepsia, his varicose veins, and his trouble with the Internal Revenue Service. She had an idea apoplexy would have been added to the list of his woes had he any idea of his wife's propensity for gossip.

She also learned to her dismay that the older MacArthurs were expecting an announcement from Jordan and Lolene at any moment, and the idea of a double wedding wasn't to be dismissed.

As the evening wore on, Lacy managed to hide her yawns with increasing difficulty. Any slight optimism she had entertained after Jordan's kiss and his ambiguous statement on leaving the *Phoenix* had faded away. When Pepe wandered over to tell them he was going back to the catamaran for the night, Lacy took the opportunity to break away. "I'll just say goodnight to Pepe, Mrs. MacArthur, then I think I'll turn in, too."

"Oh, I understand, honey. Being out on the water all day pure takes the starch out of a body. I guess Jordan will want to be with Lo, if Horace ever lets him loose, so you just run along and don't worry about me. I'm going to go below before I fall asleep here in this deck chair."

Naylor and Lolene had disappeared by the time Lacy accompanied Pepe down to the floating dock where he had left his rubber raft. "I don't want to stay here, darn it," she grumbled.

"Then don't."

She eyed him doubtfully. "Do you think anyone would care if I went back to the *Phoenix?*"

"*Pequena,* who should care? Your friend Jordan will be well taken care of by his lady friend, so why not suit yourself? No one will be interested in where you spend the night—unless it is myself, but then you have already broken my poor heart. I'd offer to keep you company but I mean to be off before daylight tomorrow. As much as I hate to end this lovely vacation, I must return my *Felicia* to her owner and myself to the University." He shrugged eloquently as his liquid eyes moved over her flatteringly.

"Pepe," Lacy said with sudden resolution, "I want you to do me a big—a very big—favor!"

Swallowing her apprehension early the following morning, Lacy looked back at the dwindling harbor. The *Phoenix,* perfectly reflected in the mirrorlike surface, bobbed slowly, the motion barely visible except at the top of the mast. Deeper in the harbor, the *Morningstar* was belching black smoke and Pepe, coming sleepily on deck, told her they seemed to be getting up steam to get underway.

"If that's steam, then I'm a cross-eyed tomcat."

"Perhaps Mr. Morningstar burns the raw material from his own wells," the young Mexican suggested with a lazy grin. "I believe the dark smoke occurs only for a little while as they build power."

Lacy shrugged off the pollution. Naylor's plans were the least of her worries at the moment. Pepe had told her quite frankly, when he reluctantly agreed to give her a ride to Cancún, that for all its sparkling looks, the *Felicia* was barely fitted out. She had declared herself perfectly willing to sleep on deck, although he had insisted she take his own space on the wall-hung bunk amidst ropes, anchors, spare sails, and diving gear.

It was the doubtful supply of power that bothered her at the moment. The outboard motor had stubbornly refused to function the last time he had tried it—something to do with the spark plug, he thought, though he admitted to being completely ignorant about such matters.

Lacy's opinion of the attractive, carefree young college senior had curdled somewhat at hearing that. She thought him lamentably shortsighted to put to sea under such conditions, but then, considering her own plight, perhaps they were both remarkably short on common sense. They'd be fortunate to get halfway across the six-mile bay to Puerta Juárez, much less further south to Cancún. The wind was nonexistent and the sails flapped disconsolately against the tall spar.

"We could use a visit from the big, bad wolf about now," she muttered, swinging her legs idly over the side.

"You mean Señor Stone?" Pepe wondered apprehensively.

"Actually I meant the one who huffed and puffed," Lacy admitted, but she stared thoughtfully across the slowly widening expanse of water at the *Phoenix,* glistening under the sidelong glance of morning sun.

Their only company was the two ferries—the smaller passenger ferry, its weathered hull sparkling under a fresh coat of white, gold, and turquoise paint, and the larger *Fronterra,* the car ferry that plodded back and forth to Punta Zam several times a day. Watching the smaller craft, its open sides under the canopy roof revealing a full load of passengers for Puerta Juárez, Lacy wished it had occurred to her to take that way of reaching the mainland. The fare was ridiculously low, according to Pepe, and she could have caught one of the minibuses that ran between Puerta Juárez and the Cancún airport, some fifteen minutes away.

A disruptive noise sounded overhead and she lay back and stared up at the helicopter that tilted and sloped away toward the mainland. No doubt it was either picking up or taking off passengers of the *Star*. Naylor offered the commuter service to his friends and there were usually several trips a day—one, she understood, to collect mail and papers from the Texas airline that serviced the area. Unthinkable that one should be called on to vacation without having half a dozen newspapers delivered daily from the States!

"I made coffee," Pepe offered apologetically, making a minute adjustment to one of the sails after handing over the mug.

Lacy couldn't help but compare the two men she had sailed with, to Pepe's great disadvantage. Jordan would never have set out with an engine that didn't function, and if something failed along the way, he was perfectly capable of making repairs, as he had proved not long ago.

As the sun rose higher, the breeze picked up, so that by the time they had been out just over two hours, she could easily discern the few houses and the pier at Puerta Juárez. Lacy, her belongings packed in a doubled paper bag, sat cross-legged on the platform between the twin hulls and stared at the shoreline. There was little to see but the thick woods along the narrow quarter-moon beaches—chicle trees, a few ceibas with their swollen-looking trunks, and the palms. Pepe pointed out several different types, but to her they all looked more or less alike. There were outcroppings of the gray-white limestone all along the shore and the few houses that showed from their vantage point in the bay looked more and more weathered as they drew nearer, in spite of the brave, bright colors.

At least there was no sign of a familiar tall, forbidding form among those waiting on the concrete pier for the ferry. It had crossed her mind that the helicopter might be bringing Jordan across the bay to intercept her. Now, in the absence of anyone waiting for her, she settled deeper into an apathetic disappointment.

"Hurrah," she whispered sadly, "I've escaped at last." Her bottom lip grew tremulous and she bit it angrily as she got to her feet and went below.

Cancún was only a little further south and Lacy managed a look of anticipation as she helped Pepe drop the sails and come alongside the dock. There were swarms of small brown boys to see to making fast and they chattered like magpies as they looked for her luggage.

"Sorry, kids," she said, grinning, "there's only this and I can manage it myself, far better than I can manage a tip for you." Her English was evidently as foreign to them as their Spanish was to her, but they took it in good form, looking her over with an appreciative grin that reflected a developing machismo in all but the youngest ones.

The island of Cancún, with its spanking new hotels and flamboyant landscaping alternating with freshly gouged building sites and construction, was connected by causeway to the older town of Cancún. Pepe hired a taxi and ushered her into the hot steamy backseat. He assured her that he was paying a flat rate for the trip to the terminal building and so she might as well take advantage of it. She believed him because she needed to. As it was, she had no idea whether or not she'd have enough for her fare. She might have to wait indefinitely at the airport while Aunt Lottie wired money for her.

The ride took them past miles and miles of empty country where the only thing that moved was an enormous hawklike bird. Probably a vulture, Lacy thought—it had that predatory look about it. There were a few tiny houses, a quarry of some sort, and several surprisingly large buildings under construction, seemingly miles from anywhere. She was beginning to get an idea of the optimism of the people of the area where their developing tourist industry was concerned.

The driver poked impatiently behind a large truck, dodging and darting in an effort to pass, and Lacy clutched the edge of her seat. Finally, he swooped out and around. She tried to compare the speedometer to the speed limit signs they passed, translating miles into kilometers, but soon became more concerned with the fact that each time their driver used the brakes he had to pump half a dozen times before they even began to take effect.

By the time they reached the terminal building, she was limp. Pepe paid the driver off and collected his own smart canvas bag and Lacy, clutching her rapidly disintegrating paper bag, followed him inside the terminal building. He pointed her in the direction of a desk where she could inquire about her Air Express package and left to confirm his own flight, assuring her he'd be with her in a few minutes.

Swallowing hard, Lacy took a tighter grip on her bag and stepped carefully over a power cable, ducked under a ladder, and made her way to the desk. It seemed as if everything in this part of Mexico was under construction. She smiled at the attractive uniformed woman who had just put down the phone and began to speak, enunciating clearly and hoping herself understood.

"You're Miss Davis, then? We'd begun to believe you weren't going to show up."

Relief washed over her. "Then you have my things! Oh, I can't tell you how glad I am!"

Lacy signed and was handed a large flat envelope. She asked directions to the immigration officer and was told he'd be available in about fifteen minutes. "The flight from New Orleans, you understand. It will take time to clear that, but if you'd care to wait in the office . . ." She was shown the office and she hid a smile when she discovered that it, too, was under construction. She took the one chair amidst the rubble of plaster and ductwork, knowing her poor white jeans couldn't suffer much more from the ever present dust.

For perhaps five minutes she studied a luxuriant potted plant standing incongruously in the corner of the cluttered room, trying to determine whether it was plastic or not. She gave up and crossed to pinch a leaf—it was alive—and spun about on hearing her name.

"Lacy, if you're ready to see the officer, I'll get him for you."

In a fraction of a second her heart leapt up and then settled heavily in her chest again. "What on earth are you doing here, Naylor? I thought you'd be steaming away by now."

"Shortly, my dear. A bit of . . . shall we say unfinished business to attend to first?"

He led her into another room, this one boasting a cluttered desk and a harried-looking individual in the tan uniform of the immigration service.

Ten minutes later, clutching the precious piece of paper in her hand, she allowed Naylor to usher her outside the busy terminal. "A proposition, my dear.

Just listen to me before you answer—that's all I ask of you," the older man said smoothly. His fingers on her arm were coercive and Lacy decided she'd better hear him out. It was just barely possible she'd be needing a favor from him to enable her to fly out of here.

They sought a shady place and settled for the tiny park across the pavement. Lacy sat primly on the dusty bench, her bag held protectively on her lap, and looked expectantly at the man before her.

Naylor looked as near to being at a loss as she had ever seen him. He stared at the whitewashed trunk of a small tree and rubbed the back of his weathered neck before clearing his throat and beginning to speak. "I think—I believe we might come to an agreement, Lacy. It happens that you need help in getting home and I . . . well, shall we say I need help in securing something I want very much."

The poise that had suffered so terribly in recent weeks seemed to return in inverse relation to Naylor's discomfort. She waited quietly for him to continue.

"The plain, uncomfortable truth is, my dear . . . I've been foolish enough to fall in love at an age when I should know better."

Lacy started and stared at him from widening gray-green eyes. She didn't know what she had expected from him, but certainly not this. Surely he didn't mean . . .

"Lolene is far from perfect," he informed her, and she hoped he wasn't aware of the direction her thoughts had taken at his first words. "I'm quite well aware that alongside Jordan, my own . . . ah . . . attractions fall lamentably short, but there would be compensations. At the present, Lolene's weighing the two of us, and I'm afraid, quite frankly, the decision may go against me unless I can weight the scales in my own favor. You see, whereas Jordan is an attractive fellow and quite well off—well, rather more than that, really—he'd never be able to make her happy. He enjoys a rather offbeat lifestyle—that ridiculous toy sailboat, for instance, when he could well afford something far more comfortable. Lolene, as you may have noticed, prefers a more . . . ah . . . civilized form of recreation."

He stared at her expectantly and Lacy noticed the tiny broken blood vessels that gave his nose and his cheeks the spurious look of health. She waited, hardly knowing what he expected of her, much less what her own answer was going to be.

"The plain truth is, my dear, we're both—Lo and I—of a hedonistic nature. We understand each other. And while we may not share your charmingly bucolic outlook on romance, we'll suit each other far better than you might expect."

As a matter of fact, Lacy thought they would suit each other extremely well. She murmured something of that nature and it was all the encouragement Naylor needed. He squatted on his heels, after carefully pinching the creases in his white sharkskin slacks, and gazed at her earnestly from pouched eyes. "I want you to go back. Not for long. You see, I'm getting under way later on today, headed south and through the canal. I mean to put as much space between those two as I can in as short a time, but meanwhile, I need your help. I want you to go back to the *Phoenix* and pretend you've been there all along. I'm almost certain no one realizes yet that you spent the night with your little friend aboard the cat."

"Oh, but—"

He lifted a thin, arched eyebrow. "Believe me, my dear, it doesn't make a particle of difference to me where you sleep. My only concern is to foster the impression that you're Jordan's current interest."

"She'd hardly believe that," Lacy said derisively.

He shrugged disparagingly. "Possibly not. Lolene's had Stone on the end of a long leash for years, but she's been smart enough to allow him an illusion of freedom. Lately, there have been unmistakable signs that she's ready to settle down, and I intend to convince her that she'd be better off with me than with a man who's little better than the uncivilized buccaneers who stashed their women away on Isla Mujeres—or so the legend goes."

"But if she's in love with him . . ." Lacy frowned thoughtfully.

Naylor stared at her sardonically. "Trust me to know what's best for Lolene. At the moment, I find myself rather embarrassed by the—uh—somewhat uncomfortable emotion I mentioned before, but I care for her very deeply, in my own shallow way." He grinned, and Lacy found herself feeling an unexpected tug of sympathy. "I sincerely hope that the acute stage will soon pass. I'm afraid I'm long past putting much stock in the deathless declarations you young things believe in."

How pathetic—to love and be too stubborn to admit it, Lacy thought, completely ignoring her own situation. "What do you believe in, Naylor? Anything at all?"

There was no sign of vulnerability now, only a rather jaded tiredness. "I believe in two things—money and power. Given those, everything else falls into position."

"Including Lolene?" she asked skeptically.

"Eventually—and with a bit of cooperation from you. You see, Jordan's interest in you could have had one of two possible effects. It could have triggered

Lolene's jealousy, spurring her on to get rid of the competition, in which case you, my dear child, would have been easily vanquished."

What the blue blazes do you think I'm doing here now? Lacy thought, stifling an urge to laugh.

"Or, as I hope to impress on her," Naylor continued smoothly, "it could have reminded her that Jordan will never be content to settle for an occasional quiet, comfortable cruise to one of the more civilized resorts. He's a throwback, the sort of man who'd rather pit himself against the forces of nature than against the more devious adversary of the business world. Oh, he'll toe the mark for a time, but then he's off again, and—" His tired eyes ranged over her, taking in her once-white jeans, her unruly hair and the pink, peeling nose. "To be quite frank, my dear child, Lolene would rather close out all her charge accounts than allow herself to . . ." His expression spoke for him.

"To go to seed, you mean." Lacy could see Pepe hovering across the parking lot. She needed to make arrangements for her flight home, and she was more than ready to end this futile interview. Lolene would have whichever man she wanted, and nothing Lacy could do would change that. "Naylor, I'm sorry, but I just don't think it's any use. I guess I should be flattered that you think I might make a difference, but honestly, I won't."

"What have you to lose?"

Averting her face to hide the sudden shaft of pain, she ignored the question. Only everything. Only her heart, her soul, her peace of mind—everything she had, or was, or ever could be had been plundered by a blue-eyed buccaneer. Her rescue had turned into a captivity she'd never escape.

"Lacy, I would much prefer to have your willing cooperation," Naylor said, his voice gone flat and expressionless. "I can either expedite your journey home, to the extent of chartering a plane and having you delivered to your doorstep, or I can prevent your ever leaving the Yucatán Peninsula. A word in the right ear can bring about weeks, even months of delay. The authorities are ever alert for a spot of smuggling along these empty shores."

The color drained slowly from Lacy's features. Her brush with a lawless element was too recent for her to discount the threat, and she could only stare helplessly at him. "You wouldn't," she breathed finally.

"Not willingly," he admitted, "but my dear, I learned before you were ever born that the world is created for opportunists, not idealists. I'd be a fool not to play on the winning team, wouldn't I?"

She tried one last move. "But what makes you think either Lolene or Jordan will pay the slightest bit of attention to whether I'm there or not?" And then she added almost wistfully, "So far I don't seem to have made much of an impression on anyone."

Smoothing the creases in his slacks, Naylor dismissed her doubts. "I wouldn't be too certain of that. It ill becomes my image, my dear, but my selfishness might just serve all three of us well in the end. Come along now, we need to smuggle you back before anyone misses you. Horace kept Jordan and Tad up until about two this morning working out the boy's future, so we can only hope he won't be abroad for a while."

"First I have to say goodbye to Pepe," Lacy insisted, pulling her arm away from Naylor's rather clammy

170

hand. "He brought me all this way—what will he think when I tell him I'm going back."

"What difference does it make? Oh, all right, a minute, then, but hurry! If Stone sees us when we get back we can tell him I flew you over to collect your papers."

Chapter Ten

Steeling herself to face Jordan's hard blue gaze—would it be furious or merely indifferent?—Lacy stepped out to the anticlimax of Daphne MacArthur's cheerful greeting.

"Hi, y'all! I wish you'd waited for me! Horace woke me up bumbling and fuming around this morning before the crack of dawn. Gone fishing! The lot of em! Can you believe it?" Wearing an incongruous orchid chenille bathrobe over her skirted bathing suit, she gestured to the chaise beside her, where a paperback romance and a half empty box of chocolates bore mute testimony to her boredom. "I never learned to sleep late, even when I was dancing in Vegas. I'll have circles the size of saucers under my eyes before the day's half done. Say, guess what!"

Lacy dropped into the now vacant chaise, grateful for the postponement of her meeting with Jordan. Naylor had already disappeared into the mysterious depths of his ship and a few minutes later a steward appeared silently beside her with a tray of coffee. Daphne's attention had been diverted by a gold foil covered chocolate, but now she looked up, her guileless gaze bright as a child's. "The wedding's on!"

Lacy's heart took a dive. Fortunately, the cheerful woman beside her seemed not to notice her stricken look.

"Y'see, Horace had this other girl all picked out for the poor boy—best way to effect a merger without violating any anti-trust laws—he thinks I'm too dumb to know why he was so set on Tad's marrying Ann Carolla, but believe me, you can't live with a man like Horace as long as I have without knowing the way his mind works."

There was more—something about Tad's joining Jenny's father's firm, Wainwright Airlines, instead of fitting into the position his father had reserved for him, and Horace's respecting Jordan's advice in all matters. Lacy hardly heard it. At the moment, she felt as if she'd been yanked back from the brink of an abyss, although by the time the men got back from their fishing trip, Daphne might be elaborating on her plans for a double wedding for her two step-children.

As the sun crept around the bridge to where they sat, Lacy closed her eyes and allowed her thoughts their freedom while Daphne's cheerful, forthright comments washed over her in a tranquilizing wave. So Jordan had spent half the night going to bat for Tad and Jenny. What had he done with the other half; or had Lolene taken care of that? At any rate, he hadn't noticed that Lacy had slipped away. So much for Naylor's far-fetched schemes.

"Lo's still asleep, of course," Daphne chirped. "She can't take too much sun—some blondes can't, you know, but of course in my own case . . ."

Lacy's eyes popped open. She had dozed off and her leg had pushed the battered paper bag she had packed her things in off the foot of the chaise, startling her awake again.

"Oh . . . were you goin' back to the *Phoenix* this morning?" Daphne asked, eyeing the disreputable sack curiously.

"Well, I thought—that is, Naylor said he was leaving this afternoon, and I thought I might as well. I expect now that I have my papers, Jordan will help me make arrangements to fly home."

Daphne shrugged and munched another chocolate. Lacy levered herself off the low lounge chair and collected her things. "In case I don't see you again, Daphne, I've enjoyed meeting you."

"Me, too, honey. Maybe we'll run into each other some other time."

"Oh, I doubt that," Lacy laughed. "I'll be back in Buies Creek teaching school—if I'm lucky."

"I wouldn't bank on it," the older woman remarked with what looked almost like a smirk.

Bank on it, Lacy retorted silently as she climbed down to the floating dock and commandeered Jordan's dinghy.

She was dismayed at how good it was to be back aboard the *Phoenix*. Almost like a homecoming. Because of the frequent unheralded showers that blew in from the Caribbean, Jordan had shut the portholes, but the stuffiness that resulted was soon dispersed as Lacy went about opening up everything. She tossed her paper sack on the chart table and knelt on a bench locker to tackle a stubborn porthole before heading for the shower. She felt sticky, sleepy and more confused than ever.

With a trickle of lukewarm water coursing down over

her head, she sighed heavily. What had been the real point of all that elaborate rigmarole of Naylor's? Lolene was still sacked up, Jordan had gone fishing and nothing at all had been resolved except that Lacy had missed a perfect chance to get home. She couldn't believe Naylor would have gotten her into trouble with the authorities. Looking back on the whole unlikely episode, it seemed distinctly out of character for a man like Naylor Morningstar to be asking anyone's help in any endeavor—much less the help of someone like Lacy. The Morningstars of this world simply didn't operate that way. Nor did the MacArthurs, or the Stones, she added wryly. She had really tumbled through the looking glass when she had stepped off that plane in Belize City!

Feeling more than ever like a pawn in some obscure game, she fell onto her bunk heavily, asleep almost before her wet head touched the pillow. The breeze coming through the porthole was warm, quickly drying the thin underwear she had pulled on over her damp body. Her stomach rumbled hungrily in her sleep as her confusion translated itself into vibrant dreamscapes peopled with familiar faces on larger-than-life bodies. She awoke some time later with a fading image of ballyhoo, the silvery little billfish used for marlin bait, impressed on her retina.

"Fish bait!" she muttered, stretching her arms over her head. "I'd like to see what Freud could do with that one!" She was starved, and it was no wonder. Judging from the light pouring through the porthole, it was already afternoon, and she hadn't eaten in ages!

In fact, it appeared to be even later than afternoon. Moving stiffly, she came around onto her knees and peered through the opening over her bunk. The sky was showing streamers of lavender and gold against a greenish blue backdrop.

Slowly, certain significant sounds impinged on her consciousness. The soft rushing sound moving water made against a fiberglassed hull, the creak of rigging as it bore the shifting strain; and the dry sound of flapping sails as the wayward breeze played its tantalizing games.

"Oh, no," she whispered, dropping back onto the bunk as realization swept over her. They were at sea again. Good heavens, it was possible that Jordan didn't even know she was aboard! He probably thought she was still in the cabin she had been offered on the *Star*, and if he had happened to find out about her leaving with Pepe last night, he'd think—if he thought of her at all—that she was finally on her way home. She dreaded seeing the look on his face when she showed up in his cockpit again like the proverbial bad penny—or in this case, the bad peso.

At least he hadn't barged in on her like this. She gazed down at her tanned figure in the skimpy white underwear, unconsciously comparing herself to Lolene. It had never particularly bothered her before, being on the short side and built more like an hourglass than was currently fashionable. She had had too much on her mind to waste time lamenting the fact that she wasn't tall and slender and elegant—until she had blundered into a world peopled with the likes of Lolene Mac-Arthur.

"Oh, nuts!" The sooner she dressed and presented herself for the uncomfortable confrontation, the better. She hadn't the slightest idea where Jordan was headed now, but wherever it was, he could drop her off at the point nearest the airport and she'd work something out from there. This game of musical boats was beginning to wear her down.

Where was that bag? It took all of ten seconds to determine that it was not in her small compartment, and she was certain she hadn't taken it into the head with her. Which left the main salon. Assuring herself that Jordan was occupied topside, she scurried out to search the multipurpose main cabin, but there was no sign of her clothes. Could she have left them aboard the *Star?* Surely she hadn't dreamed bringing them back with her and tossing them . . .

The chart table! She searched on it and under it and inside the various compartments, all to no avail. The bag was simply missing! She was stuck here in her bra and panties, unless . . .

Spinning around with a determined jut to her chin, she yanked open the door to Jordan's cabin and marched to the locker. Passing over the cotton outfits she had worn before, she reached for one of the handsome ensembles of trousers and matching safari jacket. The discreet label bore Jordan's name as well as that of his tailor and she hoped they were priceless— judging from both look and feel, the material had to be raw silk.

Ruthlessly she tugged the pants on; they were loose in the middle and snug at the hips, pointing up one of the basic differences in their builds. She tied the pants at the waist with a foulard tie before buttoning herself into the jacket and rolling the sleeves up. Standing on tiptoe before the small mirror, she wrinkled her nose in dismay. The gesture might be worth it, but the effect was hardly what she had expected. She folded the lapels inward to disguise the cleavage and turned toward the door with a militant expression.

Him and his cute games! He thought it amusing to steal her clothes and hide them, did he? Well, she hoped he'd be amused when he saw her wearing his raw silk leisure clothes. She'd have taken the dinner jacket except she didn't fancy wool against her skin.

It was as though he'd been expecting her all along.

Sprawling there at the tiller, one bronzed arm stretched out to the nearby sheets, he grinned lazily at her as his shuttered eyes roamed over her attire. "Had a good nap?"

Her eyes blazed. "What do you think you're up to now, Jordan? Haven't you had enough of your silly little games?"

"Calm down, honey—what games are you talking about?" he asked mildly.

"You know what games! The very idea of hiding my clothes! That's the most—the most *juvenile* thing I've ever heard of!"

"You misunderstand me," he reasoned as her fury increased in proportion to his calmness. "I'm not playing games, sweetheart—although I'm perfectly willing to. I'm just assuring myself that you won't jump ship the first chance you get and take off again. I can't see you charging into an airport dressed in something like that and demanding a ticket home." His eyes, no longer shuttered now, gleamed appreciatively, and following their course, Lacy grabbed the lapels that had drooped to reveal twin areas of milky white skin.

Standing up suddenly, Jordan moved toward her and Lacy stiffened, but he only eased past her and leapt nimbly up to where he could reach the main halyard. "Drop the jib for me, will you? We've lost the wind, anyway."

At a complete loss, Lacy could only do as he asked. That much she had learned between sailing on board the *Phoenix* and the *Felicia*, at least. Her baggy clothes got in the way and she rubbed her elbows impatiently against her waist in an effort to shove her sleeves out of the way as she eased the jib halyard through her hands. It was easy to see how Jordan had come by the calluses he sported.

By the time she had completed the job, Jordan had

winched down the bow anchor, and he allowed the sloop to swing with the current. From high on the bow Lacy watched him drop down into the cockpit, and as she stood there uncertainly, her anger drained away by the brief flurry of activity, only to be replaced by a less easily definable emotion, she heard her stomach growl emptily.

Oh, heavens, it was hopeless! Here she was in the midst of a Hollywood-style melodrama—kidnapped on the high seas as the sun settled over a Technicolor ocean, the hero in his close-fitting jeans and open shirt turning to eye her speculatively, and all she could think of was *food!*

"Hungry?" Jordan called softly, reading her mind with disconcerting accuracy, and she burst out laughing. The whole affair was so—so ludicrous! Perhaps there was hope for her survival after all. It seemed that a broken heart wasn't going to affect either her sense of humor or her appetite.

She climbed down, taking care not to trip on her rapidly unfolding pants legs. "I'd better try something else. This outfit has too much silk in it to stay put."

He allowed her to precede him into the companionway. "I'd say it has distinct possibilities then," he suggested wickedly.

"Jordan, stop it! Anyway, I don't know what on earth you're playing at this time, but I do hope you took time to restock. There was darned little to eat around here the last time I looked."

"Oh, I don't think you'll be too disappointed," he assured her mockingly. "My end of the deal included a complete restocking with all essentials, among other considerations."

She halted abruptly and he slammed into her back. "What deal?" she demanded, turning to glare at him suspiciously.

"Nothing to concern yourself with, honey. Now, how about some *camarones* in a garlic sauce and perhaps a—"

"Jordan! I insist on—"

"You talk too much, sugar. There's only one surefire way to shut you up, isn't there?" He covered her outraged gasp with a determined mouth and she was helpless against the flood of feelings that swept over her.

As his mouth lifted to move seductively to her nose, her eyes, and the pulse spots just under her jaw, she gave up and allowed her hands the freedom they demanded. They moved to the thick vital hair that grew to a point on his nape and then, when his lips invaded the open front of her jacket, she gasped and her fingers curled convulsively.

"Food will have to wait," Jordan muttered gruffly into the skin of her warm throat, and he swung her up into his arms, barely missing the chart table, and headed for his cabin. Once there, he deposited her onto his wide bunk and waited only long enough to divest himself of his clothes before joining her. "If you starve to death, woman, on your head be it," he growled, gathering her against him as soon as he shucked the jacket from her shoulders and unknotted his silk tie from her waist.

The bagging trousers served to hold her prisoner as his leg came over her hips. She twisted and found herself hopelessly entangled in the silky beige fabric and he grabbed a handful and pulled her back against him, laughing huskily at her helplessness. "I warned you," he whispered.

"Jordan—maybe we'd better eat now. Aren't you hungry?" she insisted a little desperately. She had already accepted the inevitable, but now that it was upon her, she tried to postpone the moment of truth.

"I've been growing hungrier since about the day after you first set foot on this boat. By now I'm well nigh starved!" His mouth revealed the truth of his words as it trailed slowly down her throat to climb the rise of her breast. At the last moment he paused, his head resting in the valley, to study with sleepy eyes the small pink crest that hardened under his very gaze. "You're like a wild flower, Lacy—shy, unassuming, and incredibly sweet when one manages to get past your thorns. I want all the sweetness you have to offer." He kissed the pink bud. "And you're going to give it freely . . . aren't you?"

She nodded, her eyes closed against the sensations he was arousing with his hands and his lips and his tongue. As she felt the cumbersome pants slide from her legs and the silken slither of nylon that followed them, she turned to him blindly, burying her face in his warm, pulsating throat. "Jordan . . . I love you so terribly much." She breathed the words unwillingly, no longer able to hold them in her heart, and against all reason he heard them.

Stilling suddenly, he lifted his hands to catch at her upper arms and he held her away from him, staring at the face she tried in vain to hide in the pillow. "Lacy, look at me!"

When she wouldn't obey—couldn't bring herself to see what was in his eyes—he began to talk in a hoarse voice that was strangely unlike his usual assured tones. "Do you really love me? After driving me half out of my mind these weeks, making me just rack my brain for a way of keeping you with me forever? Oh, woman!" he groaned, hauling her ruthlessly up against his rock-hard body. "Oh, sweetheart," he sighed into her hair as his hands began their unconscious seduction of her flesh by curving her against him, rounding her cool white hips to press her to his demanding body.

Over the rushing sound of her own pulses, the ragged breath that was forced from her lungs, Lacy heard the love words she had despaired of ever hearing. Jordan poured them freely into her hair, her ears, her lips as if he too had been bottling them up.

Capturing her hands, he kissed each fingertip and then placed them on his body, guiding them even as he told her softly that he would never let her go once she was his. "If you only knew, precious, the time I've had trying to find a way to keep you here once you had your papers. I want to take you directly to Mobile—although North Carolina's possible, if you insist."

She leaned away from him to blink in bewilderment. "Jordan, what on earth are you talking about?"

He closed her eyes with a kiss. "The marriage laws, love. Mobile's closer, but your aunt's in North Carolina. Neither place has a waiting period. And speaking of waiting periods . . ." Once more he lowered his mouth to her waiting lips and the kiss lengthened into a giving and a taking that was beyond anything Lacy had ever experienced. As his lips moved down her body, Lacy reeled with the exquisite sensations he was bringing forth in the wake of his hands and his lips.

He guided her skillfully, tenderly into the realms of physical love and waited until she was soaring before allowing his own control to break. Together they drifted slowly back to earth, wrapped in a warm, golden ambience. Jordan did not release her, but as she began to stir, he drew her even closer to him and whispered reassuring love words against her damp face.

After a while, he smiled ruefully. "From the sublime to the ridiculous, love, but I'm hungry. Are you?"

"Starved!"

They sampled the shrimp from Naylor's chef, with the accompanying highly spiced sauce, and Jordan insisted on feeding her succulent morsels, threatening her when she ignored the tiny shrimp to nip at his finger.

"I'm going to have to work on your taste in wine," he warned her as she wrinkled her nose at an astringent Chablis.

"What about my taste in clothes?" she gurgled, looking down in chagrin at the navy silk pajamas that fitted like a circus tent.

"My mother's taste in nightwear. She'll be delighted they're not going to waste after all."

Sobering, Lacy said, "Jordan—will your folks be disappointed that you aren't marrying Lolene? You mentioned your father's hopes to rejoin the two families—or was that Daphne?"

"Been listening to gossip?" He finished his wine and lighted one of his thin dark cheroots and Lacy tucked her bare feet up under her on the cushioned locker.

"The Stones and MacArthurs started out in business together some forty-five years ago, when both Horace and Dad were single. They were hardly out of school at the time, but between them they lucked onto something successful and the Stone-MacArthur Emporiums were born. Somewhere along the line they began to grow up into different attitudes. Horace married a socialite who, incidentally, produced Lolene, and Dad married my mother, a small-town Louisiana girl who baked the world's best cracklin' cornbread. Fourteen Jay Stone branches later, she still does."

"And Horace?" Lacy prompted softly after Jordan had poured them both sherry, making hers creme as opposed to his own dry.

"Horace decided he'd have a fling at cattle raising and a few other traditional Texas enterprises, including oil. He divorced Lo's mother and married twice more— he has good taste in wives, actually—I've liked them all. Heaven knows, for all her empty-headedness, there's not a malicious bone in Daphne's body. But that doesn't concern us, my little Lacy girl. Except for Dad and Horace getting together at Palm Springs for golf a couple of times a year, the families pretty much go their separate ways. Oh, I'll admit I've spent a few odd weekends with Lo or Tad from time to time and it occurred to me when the pressure to marry began rising too fast for comfort that Lo would be as good a candidate as any for wife of the CEO of Stone, Inc."

"Who put on the pressure, Lolene or your father?"

"Actually," he said, grinning, "it was Mother. She has some idea about grandchildren, and since I'm the only source of those . . ." He shrugged expressively and Lacy stared at her toes under the edges of the navy silk. "Your turn now," he commanded tenderly.

She raised a face that was slightly pale with resolution. It had to come out sometime. "Jordan, I'm afraid it's not good," she began. "You see—I was born after my mother had been married two months." She presented the facts baldly and waited for his reaction. When it didn't come, she tilted her head in puzzlement. "Don't you know what I mean? I'm the next thing to illegitimate!"

He frowned and she winced away from his sudden anger. It was the last thing she had expected—disgust, perhaps, or even sympathy, but hardly anger.

"Good heavens, girl, have you been holding that against your poor mother all these years? I would have thought better of you!"

She crumpled. Turning her head to one side, she rested it on her clasped knees and willed the tears to subside. She was more hurt than she would have thought possible, wanting only Jordan's good opinion of her, regardless of her parents' action.

"Lacy—darling. Don't cry," he urged, scooping her up to nestle her on his lap. "I have an idea there's more to it than you've just told me. Otherwise you wouldn't have reacted the way you did whenever I threatened to get in under your guard. Come on, now—once we get all the sorting out behind us, we're going to be making the slowest cruise on record between here and the States. It'll be a sort of prehoneymoon honeymoon, you might say." He turned her so that her head was tucked up under the protection of his aggressive jaw and his fingers began to play idly with the pearl buttons of her pajama top.

The telling wasn't as bad as she had expected. In plain, unadorned phrases, she told him of the constant fights between her parents up to the final one, when neither of them wanted to assume responsibility for the child they had created between them.

"Darling, it sounds bad, but as tragic as it was, it's all behind you now. At any rate, I warn you—I come from a long line of disgustingly happy marriages. There are plenty of those around, you know, although they seldom make the headlines."

Her arms crept inside his shirt and as the fingers of one hand tucked cozily inside the back of his belt, the others combed through the pelt of wiry curls on his chest, discovering, to her delight, the tiny hardened points of his nipples.

"You'd better know what you're doing, honey," he growled in her ear, "because that's the quickest method on record of ending a conversation."

She snatched back her hand only to have it captured and replaced firmly inside his shirt. "But, Jordan, what went on between you and Naylor—did you have some sort of a deal?"

His breath was expelled in a heavy sigh of impatience. "To put it bluntly, I traded him something I didn't want for something I did. When I discovered you'd gone again—oh, yes, you didn't think I'd be that careless, did you? Anyway, I had promised the boy to talk to Horace about letting him off the hook, with regards to both his future work and the Wainwright girl, and by the time I got free, I found out you'd jumped ship. I figured you'd just decided to sleep aboard the *Phoenix*, but when I saw you and Palanco, heading off across the bay, I blew a gasket."

"Poor Pepe," Lacy murmured against the throbbing warmth of Jordan's chest.

"Poor Pepe, my eye—he's lucky to have got off in one piece. I had to take off for a few hours to cool down, but that was only after Naylor and I struck a bargain—he'd fetch you back with the copter using any ruse he could come up with, and restock our supplies to boot, and I'd get out of his way as far as Lo was concerned."

"Which makes you an even bigger pirate than you accused Naylor of being," she pointed out.

"Sweetheart, when the stakes are this high, I'd put Jean Lafitte in the shade," he growled, and then, having somehow managed to lay open her pajama top, he cupped her breasts in the palms of his hands, gazing down at them with swiftly darkening eyes. "Do you fancy a seagoing honeymoon?"

"I fancy anything, anywhere, as long as you're there," she told him softly, reaching for the buttons on his shirt.

"That pretty well seals our mutual fate, then. We might need a bigger boat and a bigger house one of these days, but no matter how much space we take up, my Lacy love, the two of us will always be at the center of it."

READERS' COMMENTS ON SILHOUETTE ROMANCES:

"I would like to congratulate you on the most wonderful books I've had the pleasure of reading. They are a tremendous joy to those of us who have yet to meet the man of our dreams. From reading your books I quite truly believe that he will some-day appear before me like a prince!"

—L.L.*, Hollandale, MS

"Your books are great, wholesome fiction, always with an upbeat, happy ending. Thank you."

—M.D., Massena, NY

"My boyfriend always teases me about Silhouette Books. He asks me, how's my love life and natu-rally I say terrific, but I tell him that there is always room for a little more romance from Sil-houette."

—F.N., Ontario, Canada

"I would like to sincerely express my gratitude to you and your staff for bringing the pleasure of your publications to my attention. Your books are well written, mature and very contemporary."

—D.D., Staten Island, NY

*names available on request

SILHOUETTE ROMANCES

4 FREE BOOKS . . .
see coupon on reverse panel.

Few authors have the unique ability to capture the spirit of truly satisfying romance. And of those who do, most are writing for Silhouette. Included within this constellation of star writers, you'll find . . .

- JANET DAILEY
- ANNE HAMPSON
- BROOKE HASTINGS
- PATTI BECKMAN
- ELIZABETH HUNTER
- MARY CARROLL

Enjoy the enchanting craftsmanship of all our multi-talented writers as a member of the Silhouette Book Club.

Start with the set of 4 Silhouette Romances listed. They're *yours to keep FREE even if you never buy another book.*

Then let us arrange for you to receive a complete set of six new Silhouette Romances every month. You'll get them days before they go on sale anywhere.

And we pay all postage and handling costs. You may cancel anytime you choose.

R1A

SILHOUETTE SPECIAL EDITIONS

Silhouette Special Editions go far beyond any romances you have read before. Because they have *more* — more pleasure, more passion, more pages. These are big, powerful stories that will fire your imagination. You'll meet ardent lovers — thrill to exciting conflict and drama — share intimate moments of tender passion. Silhouette Special Editions keep you entranced as you turn each page.

4 Silhouette Special Editions FREE — no strings attached

Now you can get the first four Silhouette Special Editions ever published, absolutely *free*. "Terms of Surrender" . . . "Intimate Strangers" . . . "Mexican Rhapsody" . . . "Valaquez Bride." A $7.80 value, *yours free*, if you act now.

We believe you will be thrilled with your four books, and will want to receive Silhouette Special Editions regularly through our home subscription service. Every month we will send you six new books just as soon as they are published. Look them over for 15 days. Silhouette Special Editions are delivered right to your door with never a charge for postage or handling — and there's no obligation to buy anything at any time.